Advance Praise for *Murder at the Zoo*

"Marcia Rosen's new book is hard to put down! The characters are engaging and you enjoy getting to know them as you read this mystery. I enjoyed discovering the world and people in *Murder at the Zoo* and can't wait to read more from this author!"
~ Cat Harper, National Steinbeck Center

"A delightful and charming new series filled with twists and turns, unexpected events and wonderful characters including several dead authors!"
~ Elizabeth Cooke, award-winning author of 21 books.

"This book will keep you turning the pages as you unravel the many threads leading to a solution. Eccentric characters, a little romance, and a lot of mystery make this book one you will not put down."
~ Terry Lucas, Director, Shelter Island Library

"*Murder at the Zoo*, an Agatha, Raymond, Sherlock, and Me Mystery is a wonderful fantasy for mystery lovers. Rosen has brilliantly allowed us to experience the wisdom and humor of earlier writers as advisors to Miranda and help her solve the exciting Murder at the Zoo!"
~ Susann Thon, Past Vice President, Central Coast Writers

"I really enjoyed *Murder at the Zoo* and the adventures of Miranda and her special friends."
~ Michael Campeta, author of three mysteries

"Love the storyline and characters, not to mention a host of my favorite mystery authors and sleuths."
~ Sharon Tucker, co-author, *Discreet Detectives*

"If you love murder mysteries and animals, you'll be captivated by Marcia Rosen's latest book. Get ready to stay up late because you won't be able to put this one down!"
~ Elizabeth Belasco, Ghostwriter

"A great read sure to satisfy Ms. Rosen's mystery fans. They'll be wanting more before this first book in the series ends!"
~ Leah Rubin, Editor, Your Second Pen

"Such thrills in the first few sentences! And what a crime scene—the zoo!"
~ Mary Jo McDonough, International Project Writer

Awards and Endorsements for Previous Titles

Winner: *The Gourmet Gangster* (with Jory Rosen)
New Mexico/Arizona Book Awards
Finalist: D*ead in THAT Beach House*
New Mexico/Arizona Book Awards
Winner in Fiction: *Dead in Bed*, The Hollywood Book Festival
Recognition in Fiction: *Dead in Bed*
Public Safety Writer's Association
Winner: *My Memoir Workbook*, New Mexico/Arizona Book Awards
Numerous awards and accolades from entrepreneurs and business
and professional women's organizations for book and presentations:
The Woman's Business Therapist, including
Winner: 2000, "Women of The Year" East End Women's Network
(Hamptons and Long Island)

"I found myself laughing and biting my nails at the same time.
Sure, her characters Dick and Dora Zimmerman are no spring chickens, but they're every bit as feisty and resourceful as her younger detectives in her Dying to be Beautiful series. What a ride!"
Claudia Riess, author of eight books, including The Art History Mysteries

"Exquisitely prepared food and organized crime ventures have long gone hand in hand, and Marcia Rosen knows a lot about both of them. Her latest, The Gourmet Gangster, (Recipes by her son Jory Rosen) is another delectable entry to her fabulous menu of excellently written books. Be sure to savor this one like a fine dessert."
Marilyn Meredith, author of The Deputy Temple Crabtree Mysteries

"Unique, clever, wonderfully written and tempting recipes...A must read for all mystery book fans!"
Inquiring Minds Books

"What a fun read! It's a wonderful plot, starting with a severed head in the sink of a beauty salong in *Dying to Be Beautiful*! The characters, including a beautiful setter dog named Watson, brings humor to the whole. I loved it"
Book Soup Books, Los Angeles

Other Books by Marcia Glenda Rosen:

Dying To Be Beautiful Mysteries:
Without A Head
Fashion Queen
Fake Beauty
Fat Free

The Senior Sleuths Mysteries
Dead in Bed
Dead in Seat 4-A
Dead in THAT Beach House

*The Gourmet Gangster: Mysteries
and Menus* (with Jory Rosen)
My Memoir Workbook
*The Woman's Business Therapist: Eliminate the Mind
Blocks and Roadblocks to Success*

An Agatha, Raymond, Sherlock, and Me
Mystery

Murder at the Zoo

By

Marcia Rosen

**Artemesia
Publishing**

ISBN: 9781951122492 (paperback) / 9781951122560 (ebook)
LCCN: 2022947497
Copyright © 2023 by Marcia Rosen
Cover Design Copyright © 2023 by Alexz Uría

Printed in the United States of America.

Artemesia Publishing
9 Mockingbird Hill Rd
Tijeras, New Mexico 87059
info@artemesiapublishing.com
www.apbooks.net

Connect with Marcia at:
www.MarciaRosen.com
marciagrosen@gmail.com

Dedication

With fond thoughts of my friends who I've lost.

Acknowledgments

My gratitude to the two wonderful editors who have patiently led me down the right path over and over again. Terry Lucas and Leah Rubin were both truly skilled, encouraging, and terrific to work with on this book. The support and patience from my publisher, a community of wonderful writers in my life especially Elizabeth Cooke, Claudia Riess and Charlene Dietz, as well as my family who I love and greatly appreciate.

Prologue

"*HURRY UP! HELP ME* push the body over the fence. The animals will eat him."

It was 3 a.m. and theirs were the only human sounds.

"I think I'm going to be sick."

"Well, do it on your own time. I said hurry up and help me. Now!"

The body landed with a thud.

Eager animals slowly circled the unusual meal.

Chapter One

Lions and Tigers and Bears, Oh My!

"*GET TO THE ZOO!* Visitors are pointing at a human arm in the lions' enclosure!"

Miranda could feel the panic in the voicemail she had retrieved from Emma, just as she was setting out for the early morning drive from Taos to Albuquerque.

"Hmmm. This is intriguing. A body in the lions' den. Agatha, Raymond, facts if you please," Sherlock demanded in his crisp and stately British manner, immediately taking charge of the case.

"Shut up!" Miranda had no time for this now. She wanted to clear her mind and be ready for what awaited her at the zoo.

It was not the first time she had shouted to one or more of the voices in her head. Sometimes they seemed so real to her. She had read nearly every book of every famous mystery writer and had seen movies made from them many times and was often absorbed and obsessed by the stories and the characters. And she loved their ways of thinking, analyzing problems, finding solutions, and delving into the dark spaces hidden in humanity.

There was Raymond Chandler's tough Detective, Philip Marlowe, who always found a dame he could lust after and distrust. He spoke to his fellow crime solvers

3

with that ever-present chain smoker's gravel in his voice. Agatha Christie was the voice behind Hercule Poirot, Miss Marple and, of course, her Tommy and Tuppence. Their gossip and ways of finding clues and uncovering secrets swirled in her head. The famous Sherlock Homes always took charge, demanding facts and attention to the tiniest of details.

There were other geniuses of mysteries who stopped by to give Miranda their "two cents" at times. Especially when Agatha, Raymond, and Sherlock were disagreeing with each other.

Miranda was sure they would have plenty to say about a murder at the zoo but wasn't ready to hear their theories just yet. Determined to silence those voices for now, she called the zoo's Curator, Emma Parker (no relation to the mystery writer, Robert B. Parker).

"Just left the ranch and the crazy lady. See you in a few hours. I'm on the road with my pal Willie Nelson singing to me."

"Give him my love, drive safe, but hurry up. It is insane here. The police are all over the zoo property, the press is chomping at the bit to get in, and the animals are pacing, sensing the tension here." Emma was trying to sound matter-of-fact, but the urgency was clear in her response.

Emma and Miranda had been good friends almost from the moment they met. They both loved working with animals. And they enjoyed watching murder mysteries, once joking with a colleague at the zoo who resisted their invitation to join them, "Hey! Everyone needs a hobby. We like murders...sort of."

"Why are you talking to yourself?" Emma asked Miranda one night when they were watching *Midsomer Murders* on television.

"What?"

"Miranda, you're talking to yourself."

Caught!

Embarrassed, Miranda felt forced to admit to Emma about the famous mystery writers who she described as "living in my head."

"You're kidding."

"Nope."

Emma couldn't stop laughing. "Don't you think this is a bit eccentric? Or at least odd?"

"Emma, you better swear on your dog and two cats you'll never tell anyone. I know it's odd, but it just happens. It has for years. All those mysteries I read are now dancing in my head. Or maybe it's possible I've lost my marbles."

Miranda really didn't believe that. She knew that the voices of her adolescent heroes from books and movies were her own thoughts—a second conscious perhaps—that helped her sort things out with the same critical thinking skills that had been used by her "detectives" when solving cases. She hardly saw herself as a detective. She loved being a veterinarian who was about to be thrown into the middle of more than one murder at the zoo.

***

Miranda's ride back to Albuquerque was along a dry road with trees and plants native to the area that looked as if they had been hung, their heads bent over staring at the ground as animals skittered about looking for food and the scarce water. None of their thirsts would soon be satisfied.

The early morning New Mexico sky changes from season to season. Colder mornings changed to warmer days and hotter ones in the summer. In October, the balloon fiesta colors the clear sky as close to a million guests share in its party.

This was *not* one of those clear days; dark clouds hovered as Miranda drove the nearly three hours to the zoo wondering what had really happened and whose body parts were found in the lions' enclosure.

Normally, she loved the drive to Albuquerque and the open road leading her away from a visit with her mother, who still lived on a small ranch north of Taos. Miranda had lived there until she was 12. When her parents divorced, she had chosen to live with her father in Albuquerque. She had told her, "Love you, mom, but I want to live in the city and go to school with people, not cows and chickens."

Initially, her mother had been upset by Miranda's move. But Lillian Scott soon realized she now had the freedom to do whatever she wanted without prying eyes.

The truth was, Miranda had always preferred being with her father. He had interesting friends. He was generous with money. He was a good father. He raised her to have strong values and make good decisions. He gave her the freedom to make mistakes, but was always there to protect her from being a rebellious teenager. He gave her a comfortable home to live in without the constant chaos and arguing that had existed when around her mother. More important than anything, he gave her the love that Lillian Scott had never been able to provide for anyone but herself.

Over the years she had become aware that her father was once involved in illegal activities, but it was left unsaid between them. One day soon, she would discover what kind of man he was or, perhaps, was not.

As she left the road from the ranch, it always felt as if memories had seeped into the land—her memories and those of others from years past.

Author D. H. Lawrence had once owned a large ranch a little farther north of her family home. Shut down long ago, a fence now blocked the curious from getting too close. And there was the Mabel Dodge Luhan house, built not far from Taos, continuing to welcome visitors. When Luhan lived there, the likes of Georgia O'Keeffe and D. H. Lawrence visited taking part in fascinating salon conversations.

The Luhan house was still a center for writers, artists, educators, and especially dreamers who came to find their voices and their truths, perhaps hoping residents of the past would somehow have a positive effect on their futures.

Miranda quickly maneuvered the familiar twists and turns of the highway around Santa Fe, avoiding the city's traffic. By now, she was more than anxious to get to the zoo in Albuquerque. She wanted to be sure the animals had not been harmed. As the zoo's senior veterinarian, they were her responsibility.

"So sorry to interrupt you, my dear. But shouldn't you be planning for what needs to be done when you arrive at the zoo?" Agatha said this with both authority and kindness, all at the same time.

Without a pause, Raymond jumped in with his throaty thoughts. *"Why would someone try to get rid of a body at a zoo? There's tons of other ways to do that without causing so much attention."*

"Precisely. And why your zoo, Miranda? Could this have something to do with your father?" Sherlock's inquiries were always more direct and invasive. His mind was always moving five steps ahead, as he attempted to orchestrate the investigation.

"Please be quiet!" Miranda yelled. "I don't know anything yet. And why would my father have anything to do with this? We'll know more when we get there. We do know this wasn't a childish prank. A man was killed at my zoo and it's damn unnerving to say the least!"

***

At age thirty-six, Dr. Miranda Scott had been a zoo veterinarian for nearly ten years and the Senior Veterinarian the past three. Intelligent, five foot, six inches tall, and slender with long dark hair and green eyes, she had been told she was attractive ever since she was a teenager.

Detective Bryan Anderson, one of Albuquerque's finest, agreed. He had been asking her out for a long time. So did her mother, who was relentless in wanting to know, "When are you going to get married and give me grandchildren instead of puppies, kittens, and baby goats?"

"I'm thinking about it. I'm even sort of engaged to Dennis Hayes. You met him a couple times. You said you liked him when I told you he worked with a big law firm."

"What does 'sort of' engaged mean?" her mother yelled. She was a great shouter.

"Dating and even sleeping with him occasionally is a convenience. Marriage to him sounds like a burden." She could still hear her mother give out a long-suffering sigh.

Originally, Miranda had planned to stop on the way to Albuquerque at the Southwest Animal Rescue and Retirement Center, on land donated by a rancher who loved animals. They treated and cared for wounded, abused, and abandoned animals—some brought to them and, all too often, some dumped at the entrance to the center. It was located on 25 acres of land north of Albuquerque, and Miranda volunteered twice a month and was often called in to handle emergencies.

It was also a place where pets, mostly dogs and cats,

whose owners could no longer take care of them due to age or illness, could come to live out the rest of their lives. The owners, grateful their beloved pets would have a loving and caring home, gave generous donations to help support the center.

However, there would be no stopping at the Center today. The shocking circumstances at the zoo took precedence.

As the drive grew shorter, the voices in her head began their chatter once again. Miranda, reaching the Albuquerque city limits, called Emma to drown them out. "I'm almost there. Try to keep the press away."

"The police, including your buddy, Detective Anderson, are very anxious we get that arm out of the habitat. I assume you've been having some interesting conversations with Agatha and others on your way here?"

"I'm hanging up on you now."

Emma Taylor, six years older than Miranda, was the zoo curator and her boss. She suffered no nonsense from anyone. Not the police, and certainly not the press when it came to protecting the zoo's residents.

This was not the first incident at this or other zoos. There were teens who threw rocks at animals and others who tried to feed them harmful foods. Miranda's "favorites" were the kids who climbed over fences so they could pet the nice lions or tigers or bears.

Her famous voices would literally scream. "*Where are their parents?*" In fact, they were now chiming in with their last-minute instructions on how to deal with this current shocking event.

"*Miranda, dear, don't let more than one person into the cage, or the evidence will be compromised,*" offered Agatha.

"*Get to that arm before the coppers!*" shouted Raymond.

Sherlock added, *"I can't stop wondering why this happened at your zoo and not somewhere else. Observe even the most minute detail—no matter how slight."* You could almost hear the draw on his pipe if you pictured him sitting in the leather chair in his study.

Chapter Two

The Scene of the Crime

MIRANDA TURNED ONTO RIO Grande Boulevard, then onto 10th Street and into the zoo's parking area for staff. The zoo had opened at 9 a.m. as usual. But within forty-five minutes the gruesome discovery had been made. The police were called and the zoo was closed immediately. The area of the crime scene was cordoned off, and everyone on the grounds who were not staff were escorted out with a free pass for a future visit.

As Miranda drove in to the employee parking lot, she saw police cars and members of the press filled almost a dozen parking spaces. When the press saw Miranda pulling into her parking spot, they began shouting questions at her.

Miranda slammed the door of her car, not that it would help anything. Ignoring everyone else, she spent ten minutes with Emma and several staff members determining the best way to get the arm out of the lions' habitat.

She directed her comments to John Lynch. He was the lead lionkeeper and knew best how to get the lions into their indoor enclosure.

"Once they are in their indoor area, I need you to collect the arm quickly so we can make sure it didn't do any harm to the lions."

Everyone was silent as he entered the lions' enclosure. Only a few clicks of some press photographers' cameras were heard. The tension was palpable as John coaxed the lions through the gate. Once the lions were inside John placed the arm and a few small un-chewed pieces of the body in an evidence bag the police had provided him. Forensics entered the enclosure to start checking for fingerprints, blood, and anything that might give them clues as to who had tossed the body into the lions den so callously and cruelly.

Miranda grabbed the bag from John the moment he exited from the cage.

"Dr. Scott! Give that to me or I swear I'll throw you in jail!" The shouting came from Detective Bryan Anderson's very unpleasant partner, Thomas Wilson, who clearly did not appreciate Miranda or her actions.

This was not their first encounter. Nor was it bound to be their last.

"I need photos of this to make sure the lions have not been harmed by this meal and I can't wait for you to give it back to me. Go ahead, take me to jail! But first, I'll gladly throw you to the lions and you can check things out for yourself!"

There were teeth marks where the lion had bitten off what was certainly a man's left arm. He had a large ring on his pinkie finger and a tattoo on his wrist. Miranda was sure she had seen a tattoo like that before. She just couldn't remember where. At this point, it was assumed the rest of the body had been consumed.

It would have been impossible for someone to climb into the cage on their own. The barbed-wire barriers at the top of the enclosure were designed to keep the lions in and thrill-seekers out. Two people might have been able to toss the body into the den but only if he was already dead. Questions swirled inside Miranda's head, along with her special voices. But it was the tatoo she had seen that was already weighing heavily on her mind.

After taking a dozen photos of her own, she deliberately began to walk away with the arm. She loved annoying Detective Wilson.

"The bag with the arm. Now!" Wilson shouted at Miranda.

Bryan grinned at Miranda's nerve.

In response to Wilson's bullying, she tossed the bag in the air for him to catch. He was so stunned, he didn't know what to say—a rare moment for Wilson. He barely caught the bag and then stormed out of the area to the parking lot.

"Now dear, you know you need to call Jacob as soon as possible to find out what they might know about the tatoo. He'll get in touch with your father and they'll probably know why you recognize it."

Raymond snarled. *"Agatha, sometime you talk too damn much."*

"Raymond, my dear, you've used that line too many times. I fear it is a bit uncouth."

Sherlock snapped. *"Will you both be quiet so I can consider the evidence?"*

"All of you, please be quiet!" Miranda whispered to herself.

Emma looked at her and tried to suppress a grin. "Meet me in my office. We need to figure out what to do about visitors and ramping up security. George, John, and the other staff members who helped us arrange to get the arm, you also need to join us."

George Perez, Chief of Security for the zoo for many years, had been two years ahead of Miranda in high school. When he first came to work at the Zoo, they both laughed and agreed, "Albuquerque really is one big, small town."

Agatha spoke again. *"Miranda dear, I don't know why you keep telling us to be quiet. There has been a horrible death here which needs to be investigated. We're some of the best minds available to you and I really think you should consider listening to us."*

"It's murder obviously. Doubt anyone jumped in to join the lions on purpose."

"Raymond, you really are always so colorful. Remember, you can't assume anything."

"You two need to wait until we examine the evidence. We cannot deduce the cause of death until we have all the facts. I agree with Miranda. Be quiet," Sherlock repeated, yet again, in his iciest voice.

"Of course we need facts. We need to look at the photos of the arm. Where have we all seen that tattoo before?" questioned Agatha.

Within ten minutes, Wilson was back and barged into the staff meeting shouting and acting like the bully he was. "We need to interview all of you. Now!" Completely opposite from his partner, he was becoming more and more like a caricature of a Keystone Cop than the law enforcement officer he had been trained to be.

Emma took charge. "We can go to the café. There's more room there." She was not about to let Wilson push her around. Leading the way for the two detectives and a couple police officers, Emma noticed Miranda was on her cell phone.

"Jacob, I need to talk to you. There's been a murder at the zoo."

Nice having a gangster on speed dial. No one could argue about that.

Chapter Three

Flinched

"*MEET ME, 7 P.M.*" *DETECTIVE* Bryan Anderson left Miranda the message. She would know he meant at the coffee shop near her home, less than a dozen blocks from the zoo. They had met there before.

They first met when he had been called to the zoo to question three stoned teenagers caught sitting inside the chimp habitat. Those stupid kids had no clue how lucky they were to still be alive.

Six months younger than Miranda, Anderson had been on the force for twelve years, a detective for four, and asking her out for over two years.

"I don't date younger men," was her usual reply.

Truth was she found him very attractive.

"He's too attractive," Miranda told Emma. "Women are always fussing about him." Miranda refused to say anymore when Emma pushed her to go out with him. At slightly under six feet tall, with light brown hair that curled at his neck, and bold green eyes, Bryan had been adopted when he was three months old, lived in Albuquerque all his life and, as he put it, "I don't care who gave birth to me."

Miranda thought he protested too much.

"*Now dear,*" said Agatha, "*Don't be so coy. We all know you have a warm spot for the young man.*"

"This is boring me. Let's get back to what is really important—the crime."

Sherlock could be such a pain!

Miranda and Bryan were now meeting at the coffee shop under very different circumstances. He was waiting for her at a corner table by a large window facing the valley and the beginning of a beautiful sunset.

They ordered coffees and Brian started asking questions.

"I realize you've had a rough time at the zoo today, but I need to know. Earlier today, what did you see on the dead man's arm? You recognized something. I saw that look you get."

"Look, what look?"

"Was it the ring? The tattoo? It was the tattoo, wasn't it? You flinched."

"I flinched? What the heck does that mean? Since when do you have a new method of police investigation based on flinches? Ridiculous, if you ask me."

Anderson grinned and asked, "Where's your father, Miranda?"

"How should I know?"

"Have you spoken to him?"

"No."

Although it was true, Anderson didn't believe her. "Did you call Jacob?"

"None of your business."

"I know he's your Godfather," said Bryan, acknowledging the distinction of the word with a capital G.

"I knew the gumshoe would figure that out. It's all about people and their secrets."

"Maybe, Raymond dear. But I think the tattoo is a key to this mystery."

"Any report from the medical examiner?" Miranda

was attempting to change the subject. Bryan knew about her father. He knew about Jacob and his close associate Fish. He knew way too much as far as she was concerned. "Forensics got his fingerprints, and we're searching for a match. Fortunately, his hand and arm up to his shoulder was intact, as you already know. But several fingers were missing."

"Sure, Detective. The guy was very fortunate," she retorted. Miranda often found herself being snippy to Anderson. It was her way of keeping him at a distance. So she thought!

"None of your sarcasm right now, sweetheart. This is serious. The guy was certainly dead before the lion feast, and we need to know exactly how he died. Some people took a big risk sneaking into the zoo in the middle of the night to get rid of this guy. In a violent death like this, the Medical Examiner is going to carefully check all the forensics, even toxicology testing."

"I just don't see him being fortunate. Do you think he might be connected to anyone at the zoo?"

"We'll be checking once we know more about him and his background. What about the lions?"

"John, the lead lionkeeper, and a couple of assistants are watching to see if they vomit or if anything unusual is in their poop."

"Sounds like fun work!" Anderson started laughing until Miranda actually slapped his hand. Well, not too hard.

"The word poop. Okay. Years ago, I told some friends we should start an organization called P.O.O.P. People of Other Planets."

"You're really very disturbed." Miranda couldn't help smiling.

"I knew one day I would charm you." He reached out

to take her hand.

It was an intimate moment, and it wasn't the first. Or the last.

"Miranda, what are you afraid of?"

Pulling her hand away, she wasn't ready to trust him.

"*Stop lollygagging and get to work. We should be concentrating on this murder!*" Sherlock demanded.

"*I believe, and I've often said it. People are not really what they seem to be,*" said Agatha.

"*Agatha, get your head out of LaLa land. What the hell does that even mean?*" Raymond was annoyed.

Bryan was now trying to talk about the two of them, but Miranda was no longer listening.

"Miranda. Miranda? Where are you?"

Her hand over her mouth, Miranda stood abruptly. "I have to go. Have to see a lion about a man."

She left the coffee shop, leaving Bryan sitting there and walked quickly to her car. It was after 8 p.m. when she texted John Lynch, "Meet me by the lions' habitat. It's important."

She got to the zoo within minutes and started walking toward the scene of the crime. Almost there, her phone buzzed. "You called, darlin'?"

"Jacob, where are you?"

He never had a chance to answer. He heard her scream. So did Anderson.

Anderson had called his partner correctly guessing Miranda had suddenly realized something important when she'd left the coffee shop. "Meet me at the zoo, I'm on my way there now."

As he hurried into the zoo through the same entrance as Miranda, many of the animals could be heard screeching and growling. Wilson had arrived, as well, and was following close behind.

John Lynch's dead body was found on the ground next to the fencing above the lions' habitat. He had a bullet in his chest. Miranda was sitting next to him. The two detectives rushed over as she was carefully pushing up the sleeve on his lifeless left arm.

"Quickly, Miranda. Observe everything. What do you see? Think, girl, think!" Sherlock spoke to her with intensity.

Wilson grabbed her arm and pulled her up. "Get your boss and security guard over here. Let them know there's been another murder here."

Miranda looked at Bryan who shrugged his shoulders. There was nothing he could do. Not now. She knew she should have trusted him and told him about the tatoo.

"One of these days you're going to learn to trust me," he whispered to her.

By the time Emma and George arrived, the medical examiner and her photographer were already busy with the body. Forensics was checking the area around it.

The zoo was lit up and getting more and more hectic. The scene outside grew bolder and brighter as once again press and television cameras arrived. Two new vet interns and several vet technicians showed up as well. Apparently, social media was in full gossip.

Police cars, an ambulance, and even a fire engine arrived just in case. Their sirens could be heard racing through the city to the zoo. When the news went out over the police monitor, the response grew to unnecessary proportions.

"You know, it seems there's a rhythm to this type of chaos. I always find it fascinating that everyone's movements are carefully calculated in order not to disturb the body or possible evidence. You can learn so much by watching the reactions," Agatha said.

Then the obnoxious New Mexico state senator showed up at the murder scene. Wilson had called him. For some reason, he was always looking to make points with the senator. Since the senator was always looking to be a media star, this story was made for his ego.

Wilson and State Senator Matthew Graham had met years earlier and each had found a way to serve the other's purpose. Neither had the will of the people or justice as their primary interest.

The press was shouting questions at the 62-year-old Graham, who was only too glad to oblige them, as he straightened his tie and pushed back the few wisps of hair he had left.

That left Wilson to once again interview Miranda, Emma, and a truly frantic George.

During the police interview earlier in the day, George Perez swore over and over, "I know I locked all the gates and put on the alarms. In fact, you can check our cameras. Maybe they'll show the intruders."

So far, the cameras only showed George closing the zoo. The intruders appeared to have known how to avoid them. Had they had inside help from someone?

"Did you kill him, Miranda?" Wilson shouted at Miranda as if putting on a show of his own. "Why did you want to meet Lynch at the zoo?" he yelled again.

"I wanted to ask him something."

"Well, what was *that*, pray tell?"

"Listen, Detective Wilson. If you want me to talk to you, then stop screaming at me.

I only wanted to know why the animals were so quiet when intruders were on the zoo grounds in the middle of the night."

Miranda looked at him as if she could kill him. Wilson turned away from her stare and started on Emma and

George.

"Emma, what did you know about John Lynch? Did you hire him? George and Emma, where were you between seven and eight this evening?" Detective Wilson asked them questions, receiving answers that would be of no help in finding out who murdered Lynch, at least in Miranda's opinion. She also noticed he kept looking at the senator.

"What's up with that look? What's with the copper and the puffed-up senator?" Raymond wondered, suspicious as always.

Meanwhile, Detective Anderson was talking to the medical examiner and forensics team. At this hour, little was known. The days ahead would offer some answers, but there would also be more questions about the two murders and what connection there was between them.

It was only the beginning of twists and turns of fools determined to set up a blackmail scheme for large sums of money, another couple of murders by old gangsters seeking revenge, and putting Miranda's father and Jacob in the direct path of suspects.

When the press left the murder scene, so did the senator. But this day wouldn't be the end of his interfering and stirring up trouble with his comments. "I plan to seek a thorough investigation of what is going on at this public zoo," the senator announced rather loudly, leaving with Carl Reed, his right-hand flunky, behind him as usual.

"Of course, he does. Politicians love it when someone gets murdered so they can get their names in print," said Raymond.

"True. He seems clever, but I think it will be his downfall," Sherlock commented.

As morning light moved across the Albuquerque sky, crime scene tape was put up around another murder scene at the zoo. The closed sign was placed at the entrance and the closure announced on its website and on local media.

The air had cooled. Everyone wanted to go home. The medical examiner would do her job as would the detectives. The zoo staff would face what had happened in the days ahead more than a little concerned and anxious. Certainly, their priority would be to make sure the animals continued to be well cared for and protected.

Still, there had been two bizarre murders! The zoo would have to be closed to visitors for over a week.

Answers would come. Some sooner than others. Some not soon enough.

"Dear," urged Agatha. *"You really must tell your detective friend what you know about the tattoo."*

Jacob, hearing Miranda scream, had quickly hung up and called Fish to go check on her.

Chapter Four

An Unwelcome Visitor

ARRIVING HOME A LITTLE after six in the morning, Miranda was greeted by her two adoring dogs and a note from her neighbor who often watched them. "Dogs have been fed and walked at eight last night. ☺"

She opened the door for them to run in the backyard, put out fresh food and water, and headed for a shower.

She was stopped by someone banging rather loudly at her front door. Fish.

Fish and Jacob had been friends and business associates of her father for a very long time.

"Jacob wanted me to see if you're okay. Said he heard you scream last night."

"Where is he?"

"Can't say right now."

"I'm fine."

"Okay, that's good. He's out of town and said to tell you he'll call in a few days. I gotta go."

Heading for the shower, again, she heard more banging at the front door.

"What did Fish want?" A very tired Anderson was standing outside with two cups of coffee.

"Said he had a birthday message for me." More sarcasm.

23

"Really? Your birthday?" Anderson was raising his eyebrows as he walked into the house.

"Could be, or not. Please, drink your coffee. Go out and see the dogs. I need to jump off a bridge or take a shower."

"Want company?" There was that Anderson smile.

Damn him, she thought. "Go!"

Miranda had pulled her wet hair back in a ponytail, dressed in dark jeans and a pale-yellow blouse and went into the kitchen where Bryan Anderson sat waiting for her. She had no intention of letting him know her heart practically skipped a beat seeing him still sitting there.

"You look ten years younger with your hair like that," he said softly.

Tears began to stream down her cheeks. "Bryan, what's happening? A man is dead, almost completely eaten by the lions and now John was also killed at the zoo."

"Lynch's apartment and car were searched. We found several handguns and fun smokes. Also, some notes that so far make no sense to us. He made a call to someone right after you texted him to meet you. We're working on a trace but it was a burner phone. So, I'm not expecting much."

"Do you know who the other victim is yet? Was John related to him?" Miranda was curious for several reasons.

"I don't know, but I've told you too much already. Wilson will be breathing down my neck making sure I didn't tell you anything. He's been really intense lately."

"Wilson is a jackass."

"Well, that's true, but he's usually a good detective jackass."

"I have to get to work. We have some new veterinarian interns and technicians on staff and some animals needing medical attention."

"Miranda, clearly we both need some sleep. I want to

know what bothered you about no noise when there were intruders. I'm even more curious about why you pulled up his shirtsleeve. Come on, you have to trust someone."

Trust. There was that word again! Saved by more banging on her front door.

"Now who?"

Opening the door, Miranda turned and looked at Bryan as if pleading for help, then back to her latest visitor. "Mom, what are you doing here?"

"Oh my, this can't be good," said Agatha. *"Someone obviously told her what was happening."*

"Oh well, it doesn't take much to figure it out. Jacob or Fish. Murders, mysteries, and now her crazy mother!" added Raymond.

Detective Anderson was standing behind Miranda with a grin from ear to ear. He had met her mother several times and knew what a delight she was *not.* Miranda stood at the door wishing she didn't have to let her inside.

"Ha! Never mind me here. Why is he here so early? A friend of a friend told me a couple dead bodies showed up at your zoo and thought it would be good for me to come stay with you for a while."

"I'll just put my bags in your spare room," said Lillian Scott as she barged into the house.

"Bags? How long do you plan on staying?" asked an annoyed Miranda.

"Hard to say. Maybe until I get you married."

Miranda looked at Bryan. "Fish."

"This case is becoming more curious by the moment. Fish told your father, who told your mother. We need to start from the beginning and examine all that's happened. At the very least, we have two murders and some unsavory characters involved."

It was almost as if Sherlock was speaking aloud.

"Bryan, you leave. Mom, do whatever you want." And with that Miranda went to her bedroom, lay down on top of the covers, and promptly fell asleep.

Sleep brought different dreams and voices. Most of them felt threatening.

Waking at noon with the sun pouring into her room, a bit groggy, and suddenly feeling frightened, she reached for the phone to make a call.

"Jacob, we really need to talk. I could be murdered next because of what I know."

The house was empty. She didn't know or care where anyone was, except for the dogs, of course. They were inside and had slept on the floor next to her bed.

Her next call was to Emma. "I'll be at the zoo in twenty minutes."

If only.

Chapter Five

What Do You Want?

"*GET IN THE CAR,*" Lillian Scott told Miranda, not too pleasantly.

"I have to go to the zoo."

"You have to go with me, unless you want to join John Lynch and his pal."

"What? How do you know they're pals?"

Sliding into the front seat of her mother's messy Jeep, they drove on without either one saying another word for quite a while. There was little traffic as they left the city and headed toward Santa Rosa and then took the Cedar Crest exit.

Their distress was palpable, each of them fighting the urge to scream at each other and drive anywhere else except where they were going.

"Oh dear, Miranda knows where they're going. What do they want with her?" asked Agatha.

"Chandler, you're uncharacteristically quiet," noticed Sherlock.

"Don't know enough to comment. Anything having to do with that crazy broad can't be good for Miranda."

"Well, that has certainly never stopped you before, dear," commented Agatha.

"Well said. I am just wondering how her mother knows

the man tossed to the lions was a pal of John Lynch?" added Sherlock.

Lillian Scott slammed on the brakes to avoid hitting a deer, jolting Miranda physically and away from the thoughts screaming in her head.

"Why are you doing this? Since when are you still involved with my father and these people?"

"Listen, love, I'm not thrilled with this either or with the idea of someone possibly wanting to kill you." Lillian never did mince her words.

Miranda knew exactly where they were headed. She had driven this way with her father more than a few times when she was a teenager living with him. The familiar road headed toward the small town of Madrid, located between Albuquerque and Santa Fe on what was known as the Turquoise Trail. At one time it was a thriving coal mining town, then turned ghost town. Now, it was a vibrant community with charming shops, art galleries and restaurants, welcoming tourists with open arms. There were, however, many out of the way places for people to grow whatever they wanted and for anyone who preferred to live under the radar.

"Is *he* there?" Miranda asked, staring ahead.

"No."

"Then why are we going there?"

"Some people want to talk to you."

"I sense real danger," Raymond commented.

"Her only option is to get out of the car and summon help," responded Sherlock.

Agatha chimed in with, *"Actually Sherlock, you are a very good detective, but you sometimes are a little ridiculous."*

"Maybe I don't want to talk to them," Miranda shouted at her mother.

"You have no choice. Your life sort of depends on it."

"Great. Now my mother's my bodyguard?" Miranda sighed and looked out the window.

Driving several blocks off the main road, then up a long driveway, Lillian stopped in front of a small cottage. "Get out and go talk to them."

"Wow, classy dame," Raymond commented sarcastically.

"I doubt if he would know a woman of class if he tripped over her," said Sherlock to himself.

Two men and a woman Miranda had met years ago were waiting for her.

"Come inside." A short, grey-haired man, the oldest of the three, walked in behind her and firmly closed the door.

Inside, the two-bedroom cottage looked like it was set up for FBI surveillance. Three large-screen computers, a couple of printers, and four cell phones were on a long table. There were burglar alarms on the doors and windows. Out back was a very large German Shepard. Miranda looked at the screens and back to the three people.

"Nice décor."

"Still a wiseass. Not going to do you any good," said the woman, now about 60 and still rather pretty, and then went to turn off the computers. Miranda noticed that too.

"Fine, what will do me good? Why did you have my mother drag me here? I mean really, my mother? That's almost unnecessary torture."

"You need to stop checking dead people for tattoos," the woman told Miranda.

"You could have emailed to tell me that."

"Nobody cares about the tattoos anymore, so forget you've ever seen them." The woman kept talking, or was it threatening?

She remembered these two men and the woman. It

had been a very long time ago. They were her father's business associates who had treated the young girl with kindness and respect. The way she was being treated in this meeting was certainly different.

"I think they still are his business associates," Agatha said in her calm and deliberate manner.

"I am not yet convinced," said Sherlock.

The other man, taller and leaner, went over and put his arm around her. "You knew what the tattoos were about years ago. Stop playing coy with us. Some people have decided to expose them again and for some reason they seem to be involving you."

"Maybe it's just because of the bodies being found where I work. I'm not sure I would consider that I'm involved."

"Take this in the kindest way possible, Miranda. Keep your mouth shut. Don't talk to the police. Don't talk to the press. And certainly, don't talk to your mother."

"Hard to do."

"Well, do it anyhow."

"A man was murdered at the zoo and dumped into the lions' habitat. He had that tattoo. So did John Lynch. How were they related or involved with each other?" asked Miranda.

"No need for you to know." This time it was the man who had opened the door for her.

"You three are very delightful to have invited me here to warn, threaten, or whatever, but don't you think the police are going to make the connection? And what about my father?"

"No idea where he is." The woman smirked as she answered.

"I think she could be trouble." Raymond was very good at recognizing bad people.

"We would prefer you don't have to visit us again," she added.

"Oh? And it's been so lovely."

All three looked at her as if they wanted to smack her.

"By the way, your detective buddy seems smitten with you," the woman remarked.

"What? She knows a little too much about you. Be careful," warned Agatha.

Miranda ignored her comment as well as her phone periodically buzzing. She didn't dare answer it when she was in Madrid. For all she knew, the police had a tap on her phone, or her mother's, or that she had been followed.

"You sound a little antsy. I think this broad is making you paranoid," Raymond grumbled.

"Miranda, you've been warned." And with that, the woman sent her off with what was clearly an ominous message. Leaving, she turned and saw the taller man turn the computers back on. They were each spitting out a series of numbers.

"You think your old man is involved somehow," Raymond observed.

"Never assume!" Sherlock added, very annoyed.

Chapter Six

A Lion's Tale

*L**EAVING MADRID, LILLIAN SCOTT* let out a huge sigh of relief. "I'm glad that's over."

"For now, anyhow," Miranda whispered to herself. She was thinking about the three people inside, determined to find out what they were up to. One of the men had that same tattoo on his arm.

"Atta girl! Do be thoughtful of courage and truth."

What was Socrates doing in her head? It was starting to get pretty crowded in there!

Nearing Albuquerque, Miranda returned the six calls from Emma, who was frantic. She hadn't heard from Miranda for nearly five hours.

"Where are you? A couple of pieces of the murdered man's clothing have been thrown up. We have to take Kamali in for an exam and possibly surgery. We can't do it without you!"

Miranda could hear the panic in her voice.

"Where have you been?"

"I was sort of kidnapped by my mother, who showed up on my doorstep early this morning. Need I say anymore? Get the assistant lionkeeper and as many vet interns and technicians available to meet us at the habitat in a half-hour. We need to arrange for Kasi to be separated

33

from Kamali so she can be tranquilized and moved to the hospital."

"It's important the detectives know about this," Agatha said softly.

Miranda answered the voices in her head out loud, "Let Emma call them."

"No!" shouted Sherlock, Agatha, and Raymond all at the same time.

"You really need to do it," urged Agatha.

Startled by their unified insistence, Miranda left a message for Bryan.

"Bryan, a piece of the murdered man's clothing has been vomited up by the female lion. I'll be doing an exam within an hour for anything else possibly still in her stomach."

After making the necessary arrangements for Kamali, she turned to her mother and asked, "Do you talk to him?"

"No, I don't talk to your father. Well, hardly ever," her mother replied.

"This whole mess is crazy with secrets and more lies. What else is there to know about these people?" Raymond asked, snippy as he often was.

For the rest of the trip back to Albuquerque, Miranda went over the events of the past couple of days, searching for something she may have missed.

"Take me home so I can get my car. Yours is a mess," she glared at her mother.

Miranda arrived at the zoo, shortly after picking up her own car to find Emma in boss mode shouting "Where were you, and what the hell is going on? We've been frantic here."

"Later. Let's take care of our lady lion. I'm concerned she may have other items inside her she might not be able to digest."

Detectives Anderson and Wilson were already there along with several police officers. Miranda said, "Good grief, are you planning on arresting the lion?"

"No, but we might arrest you. Where have you been?" Bryan was being Detective Anderson and was very annoyed she had disappeared for so many hours.

"*The detective is watching you. That might not be good,*" observed Sherlock.

"*You never think anything is good,*" Raymond snapped at him.

"I had to go somewhere with my dear, loving mother."

"Forgive me for saying so *love*, but you're full of it at this point," Bryan commented as he walked next to her while she headed for the zoo hospital.

"No time for you, *love*," she snapped at him and started to walk away. Thinking better of it, she decided to explain what she was about to do.

"This procedure is complicated. In fact, it's a very delicate and detailed process when taking any animal for tests or surgery. Kamali will be anesthetized and have various tests including ultrasound scans and x-rays as well as having blood samples drawn. Protecting Kamali, keeping her safe, and making sure she doesn't wake up during any of it, is essential. It takes a team of professionals who care a lot for animals to accomplish this and ensure a safe outcome. So, I don't need you or your partner breathing down my neck or being a nuisance. Now, get out of my way, and let me do my job!"

A short while later, the entire team in the surgical area remained quiet as Miranda was examining the lioness, not sure what was happening. Then Miranda suddenly burst out laughing as she was checking Kamali.

"Our lady lion has quite a tale to tell. She's pregnant!"

New births at the zoo were always a time of anticipation and excitement. They gave continued hope for the survival of their species and much joy to the zoo staff and visitors.

"It feels like she'll probably give birth to at least two or three cubs in a few months."

The scans and x-rays showed no other large pieces of clothing, however Kamali was given some mild medication to make her vomit. She would eventually provide a few more scraps of clothing and several pieces of paper like the ones in John Lynch's apartment. No one knew what they meant.

Not yet.

A pregnant Kamali was great news for the zoo, taking away at least a little of the sting from the recent bad press. Kasi, the soon-to-be father, seemed to be roaming around with a bit of a superior attitude.

It was the next morning when Jacob finally answered Miranda's call about being frightened and thinking she might be next in line to be murdered.

"I'm sorry, really I am, but for now I can't meet. Do be careful. Listen to what you were told by the charming people in Madrid. And we'll be watching out for you. I promise."

Before she could reply, he hung up and her mother walked in to announce, "Miranda, your friend Dennis stopped by last night. We had such a lovely chat. What a nice man."

"Good, mom, you marry him."

"Where were you so late?"

"With Emma, checking on Kamali, the lion we have in the hospital. We're keeping her there overnight just to be safe. Then we went to dinner to discuss our mutual dilemmas."

Mother, you're one of them. When are you going home?

Miranda was thinking to herself.

"Did you tell anyone where you went the other day?

"No."

"Did you tell Dennis when he stopped by?

"No."

"You know she's lying."

Raymond had that right.

Chapter Seven

Southwest Rescue and Retirement Center

*L**IES WILL BRING YOU* down. Miranda's father had talked to her about lies and lying twenty years ago when she was telling the lies many teenagers think they can get away with, like going out late at night to meet her high school sweetheart.

"Where were you?" Her father had asked.

"I was here."

"Really. I sure didn't see you anywhere in the house. Your dog was looking for you too."

"Okay, I went out to meet Jimmy."

"Well, I hope it was worth it. Remember what I told you about lying. It sneaks into your soul and hurts your self-respect."

"Dad, now I told you the truth. Okay?"

"Of course, it's okay. And, of course, you're grounded for the next two weeks."

What was both amazing and annoying to Miranda about it was he said it with a huge smile.

Now, twenty years later, she was remembering those conversations and wondering about his truths. He had many meetings in their home with some strange characters, a few who had odd nicknames. Sometimes she overheard (intentionally of course) their conversations and wondered how legal their business activities were.

She felt like she was lying a lot lately. She had lied to Dennis about how she felt about him. She lied to Bryan about Jacob and Fish...and, of course, about those damn tattoos.

Agatha reflected, *"There must be a good reason."*

Too many thoughts were swirling in her head. She was getting ready to go to another emergency, this time at the Southwest Animal Rescue and Retirement Center. A rancher's horse had been badly injured.

The Center's Director had called and literally pleaded, "Miranda, please can you get here soon? We have a horse in terrible pain and the rancher is devastated. It was an accident. He backed into his horse with a tractor. He didn't realize she was behind him."

"Give me an hour." It was four days since the first body was found at the zoo. There was an ongoing police investigation but no one at the zoo was being told what was happening with it.

"The cops don't trust you to tell it to them straight. They think you got something to hide." said Raymond.

Packing up her medical supplies and rushing to leave, Miranda shouted to Emma at the last minute, "Come with me! You need a break from all the craziness here for a few hours."

It would turn out to be much longer.

The criminals and the crazies, they all seemed to want a piece of Miranda.

Chapter Eight

The Senator and His Flunky

*W*HILE MIRANDA AND EMMA were on their way to the Rescue Center, Senator Matthew Graham was giving an impromptu press conference about the zoo murders. His right-hand man (or better know as his right-hand flunky) Carl Reed, a year older than Graham but years younger in behavior, was standing next to him.

Senator Graham and Carl Reed served each other's egos and purposes. They met when Graham first got into politics years earlier. His climb from city councilman to state senator was built on a reputation of being someone who helped his community and his state. However, much of what he accomplished was through back door maneuvering and help from Reed. His life was very much about dirty politics.

As soon as the zoo's Media Manger, Deidre Carter heard about the conference she called Emma to turn on the radio. "Two murders at the Albuquerque Zoo and where is the Senior Veterinarian and Curator? They're off to play with a horse at the animal center miles out of town instead of helping the police with their investigation. It's disgraceful!"

"He is such a jerk and troublemaker. I'll respond when I get back." Emma was livid.

You could almost see Sherlock pacing, while joining the conversation.

"Idiot Senator. He's going to put you in danger."

It was late morning as they headed to the Center and Miranda noticed that the endless drought continued to take its toll on the landscape. They passed a dilapidated building that was once a popular bar, ranches, farmland with grazing cattle, and a couple of small Indian casinos.

Still, the sun could be seen blazing on the distant mountains in Santa Fe and on the Sandia's framing Albuquerque. "It always feels like this land hides so much mystery," Emma said, watching the miles pass by, not wanting to think about the mess she would have later with the media.

Miranda drove into the Center. At the entrance there was a huge welcome sign made of light-colored wood, its name painted in colors of rust, orange, teal, and yellow. The director was waiting to take her to the animal surgery building. The distraught owner was sitting on a bench outside the building.

Emma sat near the man, put her arm around him, telling him his horse was in good hands. Tears were streaming down his face, and he was fearing the worst. "It was an accident. I never saw her. I never saw her!"

When Miranda came out to ask him a couple questions about the horse and the accident, Emma stepped aside to call Deidre. "What is the fallout from Senator Jackass's press conference?"

"At least half a dozen calls from the local media asking for your response. I told them you plan to have a statement later addressing the senators inflammatory and untrue remarks." Deidre Carter was a pro at her job. She had been at it for over a dozen years.

"Thanks, we'll be back by late afternoon."

The huge gash Miranda saw on the left side of a beautiful young horse was at least four inches long and two inches wide, her insides staring at Miranda as she and the Center's medical staff anesthetized the animal. She was grateful it wasn't on one of her legs forcing Miranda to put the horse down.

Nearly two hours later, the rancher went over and hugged Miranda. She told him, "Your horse is doing well, but I want her to remain here until all her vital signs are stable. The Center staff will watch over her and call me to come back if there's any serious change in her condition."

They were soon going to be thanking him.

Senator Graham's press stunt had, indeed, inspired a few crazies. Getting in her van, Miranda checked her phone messages, one of them from Fish.

"Jacob said be very careful. The senator may possibly put you in danger." Click. He certainly was a man of few words!

The voices seemed to be talking all at once.

"Why is Jacob so worried? Does he know something?" asked Agatha.

"Sure, he does. He knows Senator Graham and Reed are big troublemakers. Remember, he knows them from a very long time ago." Even Raymond and Sherlock sounded worried.

Bishop Garrett, whose horse had been hurt, was also getting into his truck, his heart heavy. He was calling his wife, "I'm on my way home...oh my god Ruthie! I have to go."

A large pickup truck had intentionally rammed into Miranda's much smaller white van as she pulled out of the Center. The pickup had been waiting.

At the entrance to the Rescue Center, the van's horn began blaring loudly. Smoke was coming from under the hood. Several staff came rushing out to help, but it was the rancher leaving right after Miranda and Emma who pulled them out of the van, shouted for the staff to call for an ambulance, and quickly jotted down the license plate number of the truck that had smacked into them and then drove away.

Both women were taken to the hospital. The van was hopeless. At the hospital in Albuquerque, the press was asking questions. So were the police.

"The thing I remember most is a man driving the truck and a woman sitting next to him. They were both shouting something through their open windows about our being murderers," Emma told them. She was released almost immediately.

Miranda was mostly sore from being thrown into the steering wheel and having the air bag deploy.

"Please talk to Detective Anderson. He needs to know what you know," pleaded Agatha in a concerned voice.

What Detective Anderson did know was that Senator Graham's press conference stirred up these crazies and he was determined not to let him get away with it.

Chapter Nine

Dennis and Lillian

LILLIAN WAS SURPRISED TO see Dennis knocking on the door. "Miranda's not home and won't be until later. She had to go see a man about a horse."

"Well then, how about you and I go out to my favorite burger restaurant for dinner and a drink?" said Dennis.

Lillian was easily convinced. She always liked the company of men, especially younger men. After her husband and Miranda moved to Albuquerque, she almost always had a male "companion." It never occurred to her to wonder why Dennis suddenly showed up. She was too pleased with his invitation.

At forty-four, Dennis was nice looking with a full head of dark brown hair, deep brown eyes, almost six foot tall, and a firm build thanks to going to the gym several times a week. Lillian found him very attractive.

Others in Miranda's close circle of friends had a different opinion.

From the moment Emma met him she didn't like him. "I think he's a phony."

Detective Anderson wasn't too fond of him either. It may just have been jealousy. Maybe, maybe not. "He reminds me of a snake," he told Detective Wilson who had no reply.

Speaking of snakes, Wilson himself knew a few people like that.

Chapter Ten

Betrayal

DENNIS FIGURED HE HIT the jackpot. The problem was, he didn't realize what a flaky and unreliable lady Lillian Scott was.

Determined to keep seeing Dennis, Lillian had told him things she shouldn't have. "Miranda knows some unsavory characters. In fact, we went to see a few in Madrid last week. I assure you, it involves a lot of money." Lillian was slurring her words from the pot she had smoked in the hospital ladies room after looking in on Miranda.

The day after Miranda came home from the hospital he and Lillian went to lunch and sat in a corner at the Range Café to discuss what to do next. Lillian was to search Miranda's computer while Dennis would contact some people he knew who might be helpful to their plan. One that would prove to be beyond absurd.

Her third day home after the accident, Miranda caught her mother looking through her laptop and making notes about what she found. She had done the same with Miranda's cell phone.

Sitting on a kitchen stool, Lillian was whispering on her phone. "We should go to the house in Madrid. These people all know how to make a lot of money."

Hearing a noise, Lillian turned to see Miranda standing near her looking furious.

"You have fifteen minutes to pack up your junk and get out of here. If you are not gone, I'm going to have you arrested. Believe me, I will. You really are shameful. Dad told me not to ever trust you."

Lillian didn't say a word. She grabbed her junk as Miranda called in and left as quickly as possibly. In her jeep, several blocks from Miranda's, she called Dennis.

"She caught me. I told you she would. Well, yes, I suppose I was careless. What if she and her detective friend figure out what we're up to?"

Dennis was beyond angry, "I'll come to see you in a few days," he said and slammed the phone down. They had hatched what would prove to be a foolish and dangerous plan.

Lillian was more than a little panicked. She wasn't as concerned about the police as she was Jacob. She knew Miranda would tell him. She always hated her relationship with him and, in truth, also feared it. She knew Jacob never much cared for her. Neither did a lot of people.

It seemed to Miranda nothing had changed. "I left your mother because she wasn't a very nice person," her father told her when she turned twenty-one and took her out to celebrate her birthday.

"How wasn't she nice?" She asked him.

"Sweetheart, she can't be trusted when it comes to money and men. Together it's a pure disaster. Just leave it at that. I finally had enough. It made me very happy you came to live with me. Of course your mother knew I wouldn't let you stay with her."

***

Betrayal of any kind is ugly, especially so when it's by

someone we should be able to trust. How often are there news stories of young children, abused and abandoned? Of elderly people ripped off by close relatives or caretakers? Of spousal abuse and murder?

Miranda knew Dennis was a phony. But she hadn't expected Lillian to stoop so low.

"Well, what are you going to do about this? They can't get away with whatever they're trying to do. I want to know what that is." Raymond sounded almost reasonable. *"Damn it, your mother is still a nasty broad, not to be trusted. You need to find your father,"* he added.

Miranda joined the conversation looking for some insight. Still seething from her mother's behavior, she added, "If I know my mother, it's about money. And I won't let them get away with it!"

"You need your father," Raymond repeated, uncustomarily like a father himself.

"I wish I could talk to him," Miranda said quietly.

Agatha reminded her, *"It's been almost a year since you last heard from him, dear."*

"And all Jacob will tell me is that my father is okay, and it will be all over soon."

"But what will be over soon?" Sherlock mused. Miranda could picture him tapping at his pipe, pulling in the flavorful smoke and blowing it out into a thoughtful cloud.

Miranda was sitting on the pale blue sofa in her living room, when she looked at the white square coffee table and noticed the notes her mother had been writing. In her rush to leave, Lillian had left them in full view. They related to conversations Miranda had with Jacob, questions about her father, research about tattoos, and even about her meeting in Madrid.

Her dogs were next to her, one actually on her lap, when she called Jacob and told him what her mother and

Dennis had been doing.

He was silent for a moment then said, "Sweetheart, I'll take care of them, but you need to tell your detective friend about what they did and about Madrid. I'm sure he knows about your father and his associates. Oh yeah... and tell him about those people who talk to you."

"What did he mean 'take care of them'?" Agatha didn't like that remark.

Miranda did as her personal detectives and mentor suggested and got in touch with Bryan.

***

Bryan's reaction to what Lillian and Dennis did was to do a deep background search on Dennis Hayes. It turned out he was really Denny Huxley, from the South Bronx. He had been divorced twice, fired from several jobs, and accused of embezzling client funds, but it was never proven.

He had come west almost fifteen years ago, changed his name, dyed his hair, and wore colored contact lenses. He managed to get a master's degree in accounting and then a job as a forensic accountant at a top law firm in Albuquerque. A fake resume with references was easy for him to set up in this age of advanced technology. He was indeed very, very clever.

Dennis had meticulously searched the firm's extensive client files. He knew what he was looking for, names he heard whispered by a couple of the lawyers. There was mention of money and criminal activities and a suggestion of government involvement. He was so arrogant, he couldn't imagine there were others more clever, more devious, or who would be a serious threat to him.

Dating Miranda, he figured, would allow him to get closer to some of these people, but Miranda had soon grown tired of him.

But then Lillian had shown up and he knew he could "play her."

As for Lillian. There really is no fool like an old fool. Even though she wasn't that old!

Chapter Eleven

A Shady History

THE LAW FIRM'S FILES on Leonard Scott, his associates including Jacob, Fish, and many others revealed a tangled web of illegal activities from white-collar crime to bookmaking... but never murder.

They also showed those activities stopped nearly fifteen years ago. Yet someone was now giving it a new start. Apparently, murder was not a problem for them.

After discovering Dennis's true identity, Detective Anderson brought a warrant to the law firm to get access to his computer and personal papers. The problem was there was nothing to arrest Dennis for. Doing research and his plans with Lillian were just that, so far.

So far.

On his computer were dozens of the firm's files he had copied.

His emails showed communications with half a dozen people back east trying to entice them to join him in New Mexico.

"This is big." "Plenty to go around." "Hit the jackpot."

There were also emails to a few local people. "Let's discuss best way to handle all this. Getting more information. I agree we shouldn't meet in person."

His secret calls and devious plans were building towards disaster. For him and possibly Lillian.

This scam or swindle, blackmail plan, or whatever it would have turned out to be was stopped in its tracks thanks to Dennis's own stupidity. Over-confident and sure of his charm, he continued to believe nothing could stop him. Miranda and Lillian would be easy prey to get additional information about certain people they knew who had been connected to big money operations at one time.

It turned out he was too smooth for his own good. Now he wanted to kill Lillian for getting in his way, when, in truth, he got in his own way.

Several emails to Lillian in response to all her calls implied he hit the crackpot! "You are crazy, leave me alone. Stop calling. I don't want any more to do with you."

A later one was an email warning sent from his phone. "You are too stupid to live, lady. Because of you, I've been fired. And the police have confiscated my computer. You're dead if I ever see you again." Dennis was crazed over what was happening.

After leaving Lillian the threatening message, he called the one person he felt could help, maybe even protect him. He had known him since he was a young man working for him. Well-connected in ways of interest to the police, he always managed to avoid jail like so many others with similar "careers."

"Don't do anything for the next couple weeks until everything quiets down. Act as if nothing has happened. If the police want to talk to you, always have a lawyer with you."

The police computer techs were having a field day reviewing the files and rambling notes Dennis tried to hide on his computer. He had set them up in secret files not very difficult for experts to find.

All the information was now being organized for the

police to review. In addition to the detectives and their captain, even the chief of police was involved. The files included the names of people originally involved with a crime syndicate. Every member was required to have an identifying tattoo on their left arm. Some members had children who later joined, and they too got tattoos on their arms.

There were definitely a few surprises, and the murders at the zoo seemed to take on a new and disturbing meaning.

There would also be a surprise for Dennis.

Chapter Twelve

Jacob

*J*ACOB HAD HUGGED MIRANDA, gave her parents a look that could kill, and said, "Miranda, can I be your Godfather?"

"Yes." It was almost a whisper.

Her parents were arguing as they often did and the eight-year-old girl, an only child, was grateful for a life-jacket. He was that and much more during her childhood, into her teens, and as she became an adult. He was also her friend and sometime confidant.

She would see him when she and her father visited the city. From the time she was nine, she spent a few weekends each year going to Albuquerque with her father. They stayed in a hotel in mid-town, always in a room on a top floor, with a view of either the mountains or the vast mesa spreading out west of the city.

When she told her father the mesa was her favorite, he took her hand and went to the window. "What do you see out there?"

"A mystery."

"Why?"

"It feels like a mystery with lots of secrets."

"You're too smart for me." He kissed her forehead and they laughed.

Jacob always took her out at least one afternoon during those weekends. Mostly they went to the zoo and to the movies. She loved films with gangsters and romance, mystery, and intrigue. Afterwards she would ask him, "Did you figure out who the murderer was? Did you think the leading lady was pretty?"

When the weather was bad, she and Jacob ordered in room service and watched old black and white mystery films on television. Those were her favorite times. She fell in love with "The Thin Man," and Humphrey Bogart in "The Maltese Falcon," and so many more. She adored the early black and white Sherlock films with Basil Rathbone and later the delightfully funny Inspector Clouseau's "Pink Panther" movies with Peter Sellers.

And in between movies, when Jacob and her father were busy, she read and read and re-read mysteries, some of whose authors and characters now filled her head.

There was always a gift for her birthday and Christmas, a first edition mystery book by one of her favorite authors. She had been reading books by them for so many years she began to feel as if they were living in her head talking to her.

Those afternoons, when her father had left her with Jacob, he told her he had a meeting.

Once she asked Jacob, "Why does he have meetings without you? Is it something secret?"

Putting his arm around her, "Darling, you ask too many questions."

That was his only answer!

Later she understood. Afterall, her father was still a youthful, attractive man.

***

Miranda loved the home she and her father had when

they moved to Albuquerque. It was so different from the dusty ranch her mother always kept so messy. A pretty, three-bedroom adobe in the Valley, it was near Old Town, wonderful restaurants, the museums, and the zoo.

Jacob and her father often had meetings in their home. She would go to her room or outside unless she was out with her new friends. But she noticed things, like small pieces of paper spread out on their long dining room table, all with lots of numbers on them. Stacks of money were placed near them.

Over the years, she heard comments. "He owes a lot of money. What do you want to do about it?" "I'll take care of it." "The police stopped by last week."

"Get those tattoos removed."

"Those guys were sure makin' a lot of money," Raymond commented.

"I think what they were doing may not have been legal," Agatha suggested.

"What do those tattoos mean?" Sherlock preferred facts.

When she was fourteen, Miranda announced, "I want to be a veterinarian." At eighteen, she left for college in Colorado and in eight years earned her DVM, Doctor of Veterinary Medicine degree. Her last three summer breaks, she worked as an ambassador at the zoo welcoming visitors and school groups. She loved telling them about some of the special places in the zoo and answering questions to help make their visit memorable.

"I applied for a job at the zoo here," she told her father and Jacob, "So don't think you're getting rid of me."

Their graduation present to her after four years of college was a car and, after getting her DVM, they bought her the small condo she was still living in to this day.

"Being an only child sure has its advantages," she

joked and hugged them both.

"I'm so lucky."

But not always. Her boyfriend broke her young heart. He teased her about the "characters" coming and going at her house. "Come on, I want to meet the guy driving the cool purple caddy, maybe he'll take us for a ride."

Miranda knew it was never going to happen. The guy driving the cool purple caddy was Fish and she was sure he had no intention of taking anyone but Jacob for a ride.

Another time her boyfriend joked, "I heard them call the big fat guy who visits 'slim.' Your father sure knows some strange people."

But she was very much in love. First love does something to you. You think it will last forever. In a way it does. It finds a small place to stay in your memories. Over the years, something might trigger the memory and you're living back in the sensual experience.

When she came home during her first college break, she learned he had gotten married. Devastated, she sat down and wrote her own mystery story, killing him.

She showed Jacob the story and he gave her one of his bigger hugs. "It's got a lot of Chandler and Hammett tough talk in it." Together they laughed. She never showed it to anyone else.

So much for young love! So much for trust!

Other things would happen to melt away her ability to trust.

On a warm spring day sitting outside with her father, each holding a cold iced tea and watching a beautiful sunset, she asked, "Has Jacob ever killed anyone?"

"Of course not, why would you ask such a thing?"

"I heard him say, 'I'll take care of it.'"

"Not by killing someone Miranda. I promise you."

Miranda wasn't sure she really believed him.

Now she was wondering again if he would.

She knew years ago Jacob had one of those tattoos she saw on the arms of each of the dead men. So did Fish. They had them removed. She never saw one on her father.

She had asked him why he didn't have one? "Not something I wanted to be involved with."

"Is it something you have to join? What's it about? A secret society?"

"Enough Miranda, okay. It's a private business syndicate. You don't need to know anymore, not now, not ever."

She was surprised how firmly her father responded and ended the conversation.

"*So, why did two dead men with those tattoos show up at her zoo? I mean, really, we need an explanation,*" demanded Sherlock.

In her gut she knew it wasn't a coincidence.

Neither was the fact her father had been away for most of the past year.

"*Perhaps he's in government protection for some reason?*" Agatha suggested.

"*I think someone may have tried to murder him,*" Sherlock smugly commented.

Chapter Thirteen

Late Night at The Zoo

"*I NEED TO TALK TO* you," Miranda said into the phone.

Bryan responded to Miranda's invite with an almost boyish enthusiasm, "I'll be over about seven tonight, end of my shift. You order pizza. I'll bring wine."

They could never have imagined the evening they were about to have.

Miranda told him everything about her visit to Madrid and about the tattoos she saw on Jacob and Fish when she was younger. Some things he already knew about her family, especially her father. She was ready to tell him about the mystery voices in her head.

"*He's going to think you're one crazy dame when you tell him,*" said Raymond.

Agatha disagreed with Raymond. "*He's a good man. Not everyone is negative about everything like you are. And Sherlock, why are you so quiet?*"

"*I'm sure something is missing. The pieces* don't *fit together yet! Why haven't the zoo murderers been caught?*"

Miranda's cell phone rang, and George Perez was in a panic, "There's been a break-in at the zoo and some of the animals are going crazy. Emma's on her way and the police have been called."

Bryan received the same information as a text message from Detective Wilson. "Come on, let's go in my car. See, I have a big red light on top, we'll get there faster. Ah, you're smiling at me, might be you even like me."

She smiled at him, "Put your big red light on and let's go." The growing feelings between them were apparent.

Opening up to him had taken the sarcasm out of her voice. She felt comfortable with him. Was this what trust was all about? Or were their unspoken feelings for one another starting to show?

George and Emma were waiting for them at the front entrance. After the alarm went off, the front gate video showed a couple of people running into the zoo and another person slipping in behind them a minute later.

It took forty minutes to catch up with two teenage boys running through the zoo grounds. "We were just feeding the animals. Why are you arresting us? The person who hired us told us what to do and gave us the candy."

Wilson, who had gotten there first, grabbed the bigger of the two boys, "Who hired you?"

The boy was near tears. "We don't know. We never met her before and after we came in, *she* disappeared."

Emma stayed out front talking to the press, while two police officers took the two boys off to jail. George, Detective Wilson, and a few more officers continued to search the grounds for the third person, but found no one.

It was later discovered the candy was laced with marijuana so, understandably, the animals were going crazy and making loud noises. Unfortunately, those noises frightened a very pregnant zebra into labor.

"Let's go to the clinic for supplies and medications in case she needs help delivering her foal," said Perez.

Miranda agreed and walked with him to the clinic, instructing him to have the surgery room ready, as well, in case they had to rush the expectant mother there.

"What else can go wrong?" asked Raymond.

"I certainly hope there is nothing else," replied Agatha with worry.

Bryan waited in front of the clinic, checking in with others on the status of their search, when he heard banging noises from inside the clinic, a scream, another door slamming, and then a gunshot.

Bryan ran inside, out the open back door and saw someone holding onto Miranda's arm and pulling her towards the parking lot. The attacker attempted to push her into a dark grey van.

Taking aim at the tires, Bryan flattened two of them. The driver, dressed in dark clothes and wearing a baseball cap, got out and ran, disappearing in the small narrow streets near the zoo.

The guy pushing Miranda wasn't as lucky. His knee cracked when she kicked him as hard as she could as he tried to run away.

Hearing the shots, two police cars pulled in behind the van. A couple officers ran towards Old Town. Bryan pushed the attempted kidnapper to the ground, handcuffed him, begrudgingly read him his rights, and turned him over to other officers. "Put him in a cell, don't let anyone else near him. I'll want to talk to him."

"Damn it, Miranda! Never scare me like that again." Bryan put his arm around her and suddenly kissed her. To his surprise, she returned the kiss. And not just any kiss.

"About time!"

"Raymond loves being sarcastic. You know. You've read all his books!" said Agatha.

While his arms were around her, they heard the beep of her phone. She had a text from Emma. "Zebra needs you!"

***

"Like most zoo's, the cameras are set up to keep watch on pregnant animals," Miranda was explaining to Bryan. "Videos show when they are in labor and when they give birth. We try not to interfere, but zookeepers are prepared to help with the birth, if necessary, to make sure the newborn can stand and know how to nurse. The first milk is critical to their wellbeing.

"If a mother refuses to nurse a newborn," she continued, "then there are zookeepers who will begin bottle-feeding them. Every zoo has dozens of employees and volunteers who help. The larger ones like the Bronx, San Diego, and Columbus zoos have hundreds of people working to care for the animals. Smaller ones like us, rely a lot on volunteers."

Emma, George, the zebra zookeeper, and even a couple police officers joined in the baby watch. Even a couple members of the press were invited. It was a great photo op for the zoo and some good publicity for a change.

Less than an hour after she began her labor, there was a new zebra foal. A photo of the mother and baby appeared on the front page of the morning paper and was shown on local television.

Miranda turned to Bryan with a sigh and a huge grin, "We just had a baby."

"This is certainly not a mystery," said Sherlock. *"In the meantime, what about the miscreants who wanted to kidnap you?"*

Bryan was speechless at Miranda's baby comment!

Chapter Fourteen

Threats

THE GREY VAN HAD been stolen. No surprise there. The driver who ran away was nowhere to be found. The man who grabbed Miranda at the zoo had been shouting, "Tell them we want the money!"

A skinny, wiry man, his driver's license showed he was almost forty and lived in Los Lunas, a village some twenty miles from Albuquerque. It was a fake, the same as some others who would soon be coming to town looking for money and revenge. After being arrested, he refused to answer any questions and demanded a lawyer.

As for the two youths caught in the park, scared and unsure of what was going on, they were more than glad to tell what they knew. One of the boys was sixteen. The older, taller boy was all of seventeen. Their parents, who had shown up to pick them up, looked mad enough to get them sentenced to hard labor.

Detective Wilson was questioning them. Detective Anderson was listening while waiting for the attempted kidnapper's lawyer to show up.

"Who hired you to go to the zoo?"

"A woman approached us in the park near our school."

"What did she look like?"

"She wasn't very tall, had on big dark sunglasses and I

think blond hair pulled back under a baseball cap."

The older boy shouted, "We didn't do nothing wrong."

Wilson, who was standing, walked behind the two boys—a very intimidating interrogation tactic.

"Young man, I assure you, I can shout louder than you. Did she tell you why she wanted you to do this?"

"Yeah. She said it was some sort of secret animal test being conducted."

"What else did she tell you?"

"Not to tell anyone. Then she gave us each $50 and the candy to toss to the animals. Oh, and she said it had to be done at night."

Anderson interrupted, "Did she tell you how you were to get into the zoo since it's locked at night?"

"Sure, we're not stupid. She said someone would leave the entrance unlocked for us at 9 o'clock."

Wilson lost his temper and started yelling, which of course he did frequently. "No, you're not stupid. You're a couple of morons in big trouble! Do you remember anything else about her? What was she wearing? Did she have on perfume? Did she have an accent?"

The younger boy, quiet until now, responded. "She had a strange tattoo on one of her arms."

Detective Anderson pushed his chair back so hard it nearly fell over.

Walking out of the interrogation room, he tried calling Miranda, but it went to voicemail. "Tell your pal Jacob you were almost kidnapped by people who know something about the tattoos and demanded money be given back to them. He needs to talk to us. We need to know what all this means."

"Someone needs to tell the police what this is all about. Your father needs to protect you. What in the devil is really going on? Two murders at the zoo. Sideswiped by a truck.

Dennis and your mother up to no good. And now an attempted kidnapping?" Sherlock's usually calm demeanor was starting to unravel.

"Listen dear, you need police protection... and maybe your father. You are in danger."

Miranda had gone to the police station giving her statement, "I've never seen the two boys you caught in the zoo or the man who grabbed me."

Both as a police detective and as someone who really cared about her, Bryan convinced her, "It will be safer for you to stay somewhere other than your place for a few nights."

Miranda went to say at Emma's.

She was exhausted and sick and tired of everything that was happening and turned off her phone.

***

"Shouldn't you call him back?" Emma asked while holding her big fluffy, orange colored cat Peaches on her lap as they finished the last of a bottle of wine.

"I will. Later. Let's change the subject. What did you decide about the new baby Zebra's name? She's so cute and appears to be healthy. Her mom is doing a good job of letting her nurse."

Miranda continued, "With everything happening, I've been forgetting to tell you I'm concerned about one of the new vet assistants. Before all the craziness started—and since then—I noticed she's been coming in late recently and disappearing now and then. Then she lies saying she was checking on one of the animals. Emma, I don't believe her. Maybe the demands of this job are too much for her." Miranda had finished her wine and was struggling to stay awake.

It was after 2 in the morning. Emma, tired too, suddenly remembered, "The Zoo Annual Fundraiser is this coming weekend! Let's announce a contest to name the baby zebra. And, of course, as senior veterinarian you have to give a speech."

"Oh no, not with everything going on," complained Miranda.

Emma burst out laughing. They went through this every year.

***

In the morning, Bryan was at the police station clearly annoyed Miranda hadn't called him back.

Then Wilson suddenly stormed out of the interrogation room. "This is total B.S.! We got nothing from this guy who tried to kidnap your girlfriend. And we still don't have any suspects for the two zoo murders."

Like the voices speaking to Miranda, Bryan knew in his gut it was going to get worse before it got better. He also knew Wilson was acting very strange lately. His temper was out of control, his behavior erratic.

Just then the lawyer appeared for the man who tried to kidnap Miranda. Both detectives were shocked. It was one of the senator's lawyers.

Wilson told Anderson, "Sit in on the meeting. I'll be right back."

Out in the hall he made a quick call. "What the hell is going on?" said Wilson sounding angry and panicked.

Anderson found Wilson's behavior more and more curious... and concerning.

Chapter Fifteen

The Annual Zoo Fundraiser

THE SENATOR WAS FURIOUS he wasn't the guest of honor at the zoo's fundraising event. A celebrity starring in a popular television series being filmed in New Mexico was given the honor. Over 250 people attended in addition to the staff, board of trustees, the press, and a room full of police, including Detectives Wilson and Anderson.

The senator acted like he was the star of the evening, strutting around shaking hands and posing for photos. That was until the detectives took him aside. Wilson walked behind him as Anderson took his arm and led him to an outside patio area. He pulled away shouting, "Let go of me. How dare you!"

Typical behavior for the egomaniac, self-absorbed, Senator Matthew Graham. Wilson turned and whispered to Anderson, "Where's his buddy Carl Reed? They are usually attached at the hip."

Anderson shrugged, and outside away from prying eyes, grabbed the senator even tighter, "What was your attorney doing representing someone who tried to kidnap Miranda Scott?"

Pushing the detective away and straightening his tie,

he replied in a belligerent tone "How the hell should I know?"

"I'll be right back," said Wilson quietly to Anderson, "I want to see where Reed is and what he's up to."

He walked inside as Zoo Curator Emma Taylor introduced the guest of honor. Miranda stood off to the side smiling, pretending as if everything was okay. Many guests were taking photos of the television star as he walked on stage. The press had been invited to a private photo session with him earlier.

Miranda's personal detectives were also standing by.

"*Why did the detectives take the senator outside?*" wondered Agatha.

"*I believe the detective has some suspicions, or he wouldn't have,*" said Sherlock.

"*For once, I think you're right Sherlock,*" said Raymond.

"*Of course, I'm right!*" exclaimed Sherlock indignantly.

Miranda heard applause and George Perez whispered to her, "Your turn to tell the guests about the zoo animals."

Miranda talked about new animals coming for the expanded jungle and children exhibits and stressed the importance of the breeding program for several species. The highlight of her presentation were photos on a large screen of babies born at the zoo the past year, including the latest Zebra foal. There were plenty of oohs and aahs and then she made the announcement about the baby naming contest and how to enter.

"Of course, you have to come visit the zoo to enter."

Outside, Detective Anderson continued to press the senator for answers. His latest reply was, "I want my attorney." Anderson laughed, "You must be kidding. I hope you can reach him. He's very busy with an attempted kidnapper."

While slumping down on a chair and making a very

angry face, a press photographer caught him at the right moment and snapped his photo. The headline in the paper the next day was, "Senator Graham Guest of Horror."

Needless to say, he threatened to sue the paper... something he did on a regular basis.

"Reed is missing." Wilson told his partner.

"Who picked up the senator?" Anderson was still sure things were about to go from bad to much worse.

"No idea." Wilson had headquarters put out a bulletin for Reed's car, telling Anderson, "The senator called someone on his cell phone demanding a ride and yelling he needed an attorney."

Fortunately, for the senator, he had more than one attorney.

The next morning, the senator's car was found parked in front of the church in Old Town Square. Face down in the back seat was Dennis Hayes Huxley, with a single bullet to the back of his head. Reed was still missing.

The medical examiner explained to Detective Anderson, "His wrists were tied. He was bound before being shot. Dead about ten to twelve hours."

"Was he killed in the car, or elsewhere?" Anderson asked.

"Definitely elsewhere. There's no blood in the car. One of the back doors has scrape marks, probably from his being dragged into it. We'll do what we can to get some forensics."

Dennis had certainly made a serious and fatal mistake.

What did it have to do with the senator? Or Miranda and her father for that matter?

Chapter Sixteen

The Senator's Problems

*D**ENNIS'S PLAN HAD FATALLY*** backfired. The law firm Dennis worked for had several huge files on Senator Matthew Graham. Late one night, he made copies deciding on a plan to blackmail him. He carefully and, with malice in mind, connected the dots. They included the senator's friends and family, supporters helping him get elected to office, and people he was associated with in his youth and before he was in politics.

It wasn't a pretty picture. The senator owed a lot of people for his rise to fame and fortune. They expected a return on their investments. There was money, power, influence, and greed in every direction of the senator's career. Senator Matthew Graham wasn't a very nice man. He was arrogant and driven and, with Carl Reed's help, he did favors for people obligating them to him. It was an old mob formula and one of his guiding principles.

"Senator, we need to meet. I have some interesting information and photos of you." Dennis Huxley was threatening a con man whose survival and reputation meant everything to him... a man whose cruelty and determination to have power had no boundaries.

Several days went by and when Dennis received no reply, his next call left no doubt of his intentions.

"I've left an envelope at your office."

Reed opened it. Inside were photos of the senator appearing very cozy with several well-known criminals and nude females, presumably prostitutes.

There was also a note, typed in red. "We need to meet before the end of the week to discuss financial arrangement, or these photos will be given to the press."

Graham's connections and deviant behavior went deep. Dennis's law firm knew it. So did the FBI.

Dennis did not sign his name to the note. He didn't need to. Reed had traced the earlier call he made to the senator.

Graham made one comment after seeing the photos, "Take care of him."

Dennis also had information on Leonard Scott, Jacob, Fish, and others in their circle of business associates. He had dated Miranda and played along with Lillian Scott to see what other dirt he could dig up on them. He got nothing from Miranda, but Lillian would have given him the keys to Fort Knox if he kept "seeing" her.

He tried enticing several friends from back east to join him, promising, "This is going to be a huge score."

Even the one contact he always felt he could trust turned him down. "Forget all this. It's bad for our business. People we know here are upset with what you're doing."

Dennis had reached a point where nothing and no one was going to stop him. So he thought.

Amazing how arrogance joined by stupidity can bring down a life.

Chapter Seventeen

Murder Count

T*HE BODY COUNT WAS* adding up. The latest murder was all over the news, and pointing fingers at the senator. The coverage read, "The body of Dennis Huxley was found in the senator's car. Reed, a close associate of the senator's is missing. He was last seen leaving the zoo fundraiser."

Detective Anderson met with Emma and Miranda late the next morning. It was chaotic at the zoo to say the least. There were reporters wanting comments, police patrolling the grounds, and several staff were still being questioned about the break-in and attempted kidnapping.

"Dear, this is getting out of hand," Agatha commented.

"What's taking so long to figure all this out? And how was that phony Huxley mixed up in it? In my day, you pushed a few people around and found the answers!" Shouted a frustrated Raymond.

"Indeed!" Sherlock agreed with him, which was highly unusual to say the least.

"Miranda, do you know where your mother is? Dennis's phone shows numerous calls from her."

"Bryan, I have no idea. You know I kicked her out of my home earlier in the week. I told you what she was doing."

Dennis had ignored all of Lillian's calls. It turned out she was damn lucky. When Jacob called to tell her that Dennis had been murdered, he warned her, "Don't be stupid like your young boy toy. Get lost for a while and don't tell anyone where you are." He told Fish he wished he could wring her neck.

"And the senator?" Emma asked.

Bryan shook his head, "He's being questioned. Said he has no idea where Reed is."

"Do you believe him?" Emma asked as she went to answer her ringing phone.

"For now, he's refusing to answer any questions. He's got two hot shot lawyers insisting he keep quiet."

Emma held the phone aside and turned to Miranda, "It's the Rescue Center, the horse run over by his owner is back at the center bleeding badly. They're asking for your help."

"Tell them to press warm, wet towels over the area that is bleeding. I'll be there in about an hour."

"Not without me. We have enough dead bodies," said Anderson.

The ride together would change a lot for the two of them.

"*Here's your chance, Miranda! Stop acting like a dumb dame, because you're not. Tell him about us,*" said Raymond in a tone that implied an or else.

Agatha chimed in with, "*Yes! We could all work together to solve these crimes.*"

"I hear voices," she said as they head north to the Rescue Center.

Anderson, who had insisted on driving, burst out laughing.

"It's not funny. Well, sometimes it is. When I was a young girl, I read many mystery books and watched most of the wonderful mystery movies, especially the early black and white films. Some of my favorite authors and characters somehow seem to talk to me. That's it. Been wanting to tell you." She made it sound so simple, like it was no big deal that authors from the grave were talking to her.

"Are you serious? Do you always answer them back, like you did in the hospital?"

"Sometimes. Sort of."

"Who are they?" asked Bryan, attempting to be understanding when he truly had no idea what it all meant.

"Usually Agatha Christie, Raymond Chandler, and Sherlock Holmes. Although sometimes someone else pops in." Miranda sounded so serious that he wasn't sure how to respond. He turned toward her and raised his eyebrows... like you can't be serious.

"Okay. Listen detective. Don't be a jackass about this. The voices, of course, are really my own thoughts or feelings about something, but they often play around in my head as if they are these other voices."

"Do they ever yell at you?" He cautiously asked.

"Tell him this is important to you." Agatha reminded her.

"Yes. Like now. Maybe I'm an idiot for telling you and trusting you'll understand this is important to me."

"I'm sorry. Really, I don't mean to be an idiot. Well, maybe a little." Grinning for a moment, then looking at Miranda. "You know I love you. Even your voices."

Now Miranda wasn't sure how to respond.

"It's okay, don't say anything. Not now at least. The horse is waiting for you." Bryan leaned over and tenderly kissed Miranda on the cheek."

Agatha couldn't help herself. *"Now, dear, that's a moment worth remembering."*

They drove into the Center, past the beautiful welcome sign and up to the animal surgery building. There, once again, sat the owner on a bench outside the building. Twenty minutes later, Miranda came out and sat next to him. "I'm so sorry, but she's passed away. Do you want to come inside and say goodbye to her? You can stay with her for a while if you want. Let them know when you want to leave."

The owner was devastated but nothing could be done to save his horse. All veterinarians know there are times they have to face putting an animal down to avoid its suffering. This time, the horse's heart stopped on its own. The trauma, and now the bleeding, were all too much for her to survive.

Bryan saw how kind and tender Miranda was with the horse's owner. He really loved her.

A short time later, they started back to Albuquerque. It had been almost two weeks since the murders at the zoo and more disturbing things continued to happen.

Avoiding the conversation about love and trust, Bryan talked about the voices. "I'm serious. I think I do understand what you were telling me about the voices in your head and how they're really your thoughts and concerns. The way you ask certain questions, you have an ability and determination to help solve problems, probably even murders. Don't look at me like I'm crazy. You know I'm right."

Miranda was shocked and uncomfortable at first.

"What I mean is, we could discuss what we think Agatha, Raymond, Sherlock... and others might do to handle a certain situation, even to catch murderers. Of course, this is only between us."

"You're not making fun of me?" said Miranda, leery of his suggestion.

"I promise I'm not. I trust you a heck of a lot more than I trust Wilson, and maybe together we can figure out at least some of what's going on." Bryan sighed and reached for his phone, which showed Wilson was calling. "Reed showed up all bloodied and said he was lucky to get away. Wouldn't say who did it. Seemed genuinely scared."

"Where is he?"

"An officer took him to Presbyterian Hospital. He looked like he was in bad shape." Wilson asked, "Can you meet me at the hospital?"

"I'll meet you there in half an hour. Does the senator know?" asked Anderson.

"Yeah. No comment from him yet."

Miranda needed to get back to the zoo. She, too, was busy the rest of the day and very happy to not think about her conversations in the car with Bryan. She needed to give a checkup to two new wolves sent from another zoo who would then be quarantined for ten days. Then there was making sure the baby zebra and mother were doing well and a stop at the lion's habitat to see how the mother-to-be was doing.

It had been a long and difficult day full of decisions and strange conversations. She just wanted to go home.

***

It was 6:30 a.m. and the morning light was beginning to glaze across the southwestern sky. Spring was beginning to turn to longer summer days, the mornings sweet and slightly cool.

Miranda's phone was ringing at the same time someone was banging on her front door, waking from her from a deep sleep. She answered the phone as she went to the door and heard, "Please take extra care to be safe. Tell them I didn't do it." Miranda was stunned. The phone call was from her father. He hung up before she could say or ask anything else.

Chapter Eighteen

Explosion

*W*HY WAS BRYAN BANGING at her door and yelling her name so early?

"This can't be good. Her father calls at the crack of dawn. Now the police are at the door. This dame needs a gun," Raymond declared.

Agatha responded, *"You believe everyone should have a gun. Let's find out what is really going on before we overreact."*

"Whatever it is, I will predict it is serious," Sherlock said firmly.

Miranda opened the door to Bryan and two police officers sitting in a police car in front of her home. Putting his arm around her he said, "Thank goodness you're okay."

"What is going on? Why are you here and why are there police parked out front?" Miranda was standing in her bare feet, her long hair tangled over her shoulders. Bryan wished he could hug her. But...

"You don't know?" Bryan took her by the arm and turned on the small television on her kitchen counter. There were reporters talking about an explosion in Madrid with a picture of the devastation.

According to news reports, local and state police believed the explosion at the house in Madrid at 5 this morning was caused by a bomb. The explosion destroyed the home and knocked out electricity for half the town. People who lived in the house are nowhere to be found, according to the police. As the coverage continued, pictures of the house—before and after—were shown.

Miranda knew the house well. "Do they know who did this?"

"Not yet," Bryan shook his head.

"Oh my god, is everything okay at the zoo?"

"Yes, we have police stationed at the entrance." Bryan wasn't sure how to tell Miranda what else he knew. He had known about the house in Madrid for a long time, as part of his investigation into her father.

"*Tell him your father called this morning to warn you,*" Sherlock insisted.

"My father called me just before you got here. He told me to be very careful and to tell you he didn't do it. I have no idea where he is and never got to say anything before he hung up. It's the first time I heard from him in nearly a year." Miranda was sitting with her elbows on the counter, hands on her face, looking up at Bryan, with tears in her eyes.

"Why don't you get dressed? I'll take you for coffee." Bryan made a call as she walked away. "She heard him say 'he called her.'"

The coffee bar opened every day at 5 a.m. and when they got there a little after 7, there already was a line out the door. She saw Detective Wilson walk into the coffee shop and it felt like the two detectives were about to interrogate her. Wilson only whispered something to Bryan and then left.

"You ask me to trust you and you immediately call Wilson about my father calling me?" Miranda was clearly angry.

"Listen to me Miranda. Your father was seen in Madrid a few days ago."

"Oh, no! You can't believe he's responsible for what happened."

"Why was he in Madrid? Do you have any idea?"

"All I know is he called me this morning with the brief warning, so at least he wasn't in the house when it exploded."

Each slowly drank their coffee as the shop filled up with a variety of people in need of caffeine to start the day. Some were going to work, others starting or ending a run or visit to the gym, a few tapping away on their laptop computers.

Miranda kept shaking her head no to the detective's questions.

"Do you have any idea where he might be?"

"How would I know? I told you I haven't spoken to him in a year!

It was full daylight now and the weather was warming up, leaving no doubt it would be another warm day. Another stressful day.

Brian kept asking questions, "When he called, could you hear any sounds in the background? Do you think he'll call again to check on you? Come on, you must know something about where he could be?"

Tears were coming down her cheeks and reaching for her coffee, she spilled most of it. Without a word she got up and walked outside. Minutes later, Bryan followed and drove her home without any more questions.

She slammed the police car door closed without saying another word to him.

Chapter Nineteen

After the Explosion

*A*BOUT AN HOUR HAD passed. Miranda had just finished showering and dressing when there was more knocking on her door. Detectives Wilson and Anderson were once again at her home wanting to ask her more questions.

"The people living in the house in Madrid disappeared. Not only that, but your father is still missing and so are a couple other people we've been watching. You better tell us what you know." Detective Wilson sounded worse than a bully. It was like he was mimicking a bad character in one of the dark mystery films she and Jacob used to watch.

"Who else is missing?" Miranda asked trying to keep fear out of her voice.

"We'll ask the questions missy," said Wilson, being his ever-so-charming self.

Miranda who had been sitting, stood up, put her face inches from Wilson's and shouted, "Three people I knew are dead! My father is missing and you're acting like a damn jackass! Get out of my house. Now!"

Wilson started to walk out the door and turning to Anderson, "She better tell you what she knows or I'm coming back with an arrest warrant."

"Bryan, who else is missing?" Miranda asked.

"One of the new zoo vet technicians. When she didn't show up for work, another tech said she left without saying where she was going. We went through her locker at the zoo and found some of the candy the boys tossed to the animals. There was also a map with Madrid circled."

"Bryan, this is crazy! Now what?"

"Police are looking for her car, forensics has taken her fingerprints off her locker and one of our computer geeks is checking her background. I can't tell you anymore, mostly because that's all we know for now." Bryan got up to leave. "Come on, I'll take you to the zoo."

"I can drive myself there."

"With everything happening, that's not the best idea. And one minor detail. You don't have a car."

"By the way, any news about my mother?"

"None," he said.

"Do you have any idea what all these murders and now people missing are about?" Sitting next to Bryan in the car was more comforting than Miranda was willing to admit.

"We're checking on some leads. Let me know when you want to go home, I'll pick you up."

There was that charming grin.

"Pick me up at two. I need to buy a new car."

***

Miranda walked into Emma's office and found Wilson sitting there with his obnoxious demeanor in full force, grilling Emma.

The two youths who had thrown the laced candy to the animals at the zoo both had identified Karla, the missing vet technician, as the woman who hired them. The person who grabbed Miranda had refused to comment on anything, but Karla's fingerprints were on the steering wheel of the impounded van when he was arrested.

Wilson had gone to the zoo to interview Emma about Karla, always acting like a bull in a china shop with his aggressive behavior.

"She had only been working here a few months," Emma told him as she handed Wilson a copy of Karla's job application.

"Was there ever any problem with her? Did she get along with her co-workers?"

"Recently she was coming in late and disappeared sometimes, lying about what she was doing," replied Emma.

"Did she ever ask you or anyone else about Miranda?"

"Detective, I think you might want to talk to George Perez. He was the one that referred her for the job. You'll find him by the front gate today," said Emma as she got up and started to walk out with Miranda.

"I'd better not find out either one of you is holding anything back, or you'll be in deep trouble."

"Would it really be against the law to accidently run him over with one of the zoo vehicles?" laughed Emma.

"Please let me be the driver," said Miranda smiling.

Chapter Twenty

Friends and Family

*A*FTER BOTH HIS PARENTS died of alcohol excess within months of each other, George Perez's two old maid aunts raised him from the age of six with love and kindness, teaching him the values of giving and gratitude. Thanks to his aunts, he was happy during his high school years. Although, anyone who has been abused as a child never totally loses the memory of the ugliness and pain they endured.

Those values and his kindness in referring someone to the zoo to be a vet technician is what had him in hot water now.

After two years of college, he joined the army, and then took jobs working as a security guard for many major events in the city. He once told his aunts, "I prefer being outdoors." They understood and were heartbroken knowing of his early childhood being kept mostly indoors by his drunk and abusive parents.

In his early thirties he saw an ad for full time security guard at the zoo. His work experiences and references landed him the job. He was surprised and happy to see Miranda there. It felt familiar and comforting.

A little over five years after he was first hired, George Perez became Chief Security Guard for the zoo. When

Emma started to ask him if he wanted the job, he answered before she finished. "Yes. Thank you, thank you." They both laughed!

Now he was at police headquarters being rather aggressively interviewed by Detective Wilson. "Why did you refer Karla Ferrell, if that's even her right name, to be a vet technician at the zoo?"

"We had gone out on a few dates and she told me she was looking for a job. She knew where I worked and asked if I might be able to help her get a job at the zoo. Said she worked as a vet tech for a small zoo back east. She showed me her resume, so I gave it to Emma."

"How did you meet her?" asked Wilson.

"At a club where lots of singles hang out, so what?" George was feeling more than a bit uncomfortable. The detectives bully tactics brought back too many bad memories.

"What about any of her family? Did you ever meet them? She sounds like a bit of a loser to me." Wilson was pushing way too hard with this interview.

George had enough. "You know what detective? I liked her. She said she moved here the past year. I never met her family. I never saw her do or say anything crazy and I gave her resume to Emma. That's it. Oh, yeah, one other thing."

"What the hell is that?"

"I want an attorney."

***

Another interrogation was going on at the same time. Anderson and his captain were at the hospital attempting to find out what happened to Carl Reed. He was brought in the day before bruised and bloodied. All he would say was, "I didn't kill the guy found dead in the senator's car."

"How did Dennis get in his car?" The captain let Anderson ask most of the questions.

"Don't know. I went out for a smoke at the zoo fund-raising event and next thing I know I felt like I had been hit by a truck." Reed really couldn't remember what happened to him after that.

The captain turned to Detective Anderson. "Dennis's death was a hit. Start checking airlines and car rentals. See if we've had any special visitors from back east. This looks like an old-time mob killing. We'll keep a guard at Reed's hospital room. Talk to him again tomorrow, maybe he'll start to remember what happened."

Walking out of the room with the captain, Anderson asked, "Confidentially, Captain, I need a favor. Let me have one of the police officers work with me. Wilson is getting out of control on this investigation. He has some kind of close connection to the senator making me very uncomfortable."

Anderson had a bad feeling about his partner. He also knew Wilson would go ballistic when he heard this request. Still, the captain had nodded his head yes. Perhaps he, too, had concerns about Wilson's strange behavior.

***

The automobile dealer delivered Miranda a new van later in the day while she was still at the zoo. It was close to six when she said goodbye to Emma and she and a few others headed out to the staff parking area. A note was on the windshield of her shiny new car.

"Meet me in the parking lot of the Flying Star Restaurant on Rio Grande Blvd. 7:30 tonight. Important. J."

Jacob? Miranda knew the handwriting well.

"What does he want?" Raymond asked.

"Dear, you know he would never hurt you. Still, perhaps, you should let your detective friend know," Agatha

suggested.

Miranda responded to the most comforting voice in her head. "I'll be fine. Maybe he'll have some answers for me."

Jacob wouldn't answer any questions after he picked her up at the Flying Star. Not even where they were going or why. Twenty minutes later, they walked into a small restaurant in the town of Corrales. She had been there before, when she was a teenager. Her heart started to pound, and she had tears in her eyes.

Jacob put his arm around her as they walked to a table in the corner. "It will be okay, I promise."

Her father got up to hug her.

"Well, hug him back! Then find out what's going on," said the chorus of voices.

Chapter Twenty-One

Everyone Has a Story

GEORGE HAD A STORY. He didn't need an attorney. Wilson gave him a familiar police line, "Go home, but don't leave town." Wisely, he left the police station without telling Wilson what he could do to himself. One of his aunts, now in her eighties, was waiting outside to drive him home. He knew she wouldn't like it if he said something rude, even if someone deserved it. Wilson surely did.

He had told Wilson everything he knew, well almost. He dated Karla Ferrell for about three weeks after meeting her and she had, in fact, approached him. He was shy with women, and he liked that she came over and introduced herself to him.

A week after she got the job at the zoo, she told him they couldn't go out anymore. "My father is coming to stay with me for a while and it would be uncomfortable for me. Maybe after he leaves."

For some reason he didn't tell Wilson about her father visiting. Later he would tell Emma.

She told him, "Best not to tell anyone else."

***

As for Carl Reed's story, Anderson went back to the

hospital to find out if Reed remembered anything. The senator was in the room with him, and an attorney was at Reed's bedside. Anderson couldn't help himself, grinning and sarcastically remarking, "Wow. Albuquerque attorneys are doing very well thanks to you, senator."

If dirty looks could kill, the detective would have been dead on the spot.

"Neither the senator nor Reed have any comments for you detective," the attorney said, giving Reed some papers to sign.

"Frankly, I don't want any comments. I want information. What happened to Reed and where was he when Dennis Hayes was murdered? And needless to say, why was the murdered man left in the senator's car?"

"Like I said, no comment." Detective Anderson nodded to the attorney then called in the police officer standing guard. He had quite enough of all of them.

"Carl Reed, I'm arresting you for the murder of Dennis (Hayes) Huxley." Anderson went on to read him his rights. He told the officer, "Handcuff him to the bed!"

Reed was stunned and shouted obscenities. The senator was furious, demanding the lawyer do something to stop this. The lawyer made a futile attempt at calming them both, finally shouting, "Please be quiet. I'll take care of the situation."

He walked out past Anderson who said, "Nice clients."

With the slightest of grins, he raised his eyebrows as if in agreement and said, "No comment."

Several days later, when he was ready to leave the hospital, Reed was taken to court, released on bail, and cautioned, "Don't leave the city."

The local press was, of course, all over anything to do with the senator. There were photos of him going in and out of the hospital, having a luncheon meeting with several other politicians... and much more. He only answered reporters with, "No comment."

***

It was after midnight when Miranda got home. She nodded to the police in front of her house, then once inside texted Bryan. "I just saw my father. He promised me he didn't murder anyone. Come over after work tomorrow? I have to be at the zoo all day."

Bryan was relieved when she texted him. The officer watching the house told him when she left... and when she got home.

"I'll be there. Glad you're home," he replied.

"Of course, he knew you went out dear. That cute policeman in the car out front probably told him," said Agatha.

"It doesn't take a genius to know that," Raymond piped in sarcastically.

"You met with your father. You notified your boyfriend. Now listen to me. You need to think like I do and help figure out this mess. Look beyond what you can see. There's usually something else behind it," said Sherlock.

By the next morning, Miranda had made a decision. It was one that would bring her closer to Bryan Anderson. But it would also bring her closer to more attempts on her life.

Miranda was determined to organize a way of looking at everyone involved in the recent murders and to the attempts on her life.

She had read and watched dozens of murder mysteries. The police and detectives often keep track of people connected to a murder or a crime by writing on a bulletin board or blackboard finding ways to connect the dots of all the playsers involved. They would then discuss who might be the key suspects, who had an opportunity and motive, who was related to each other. Miranda figured, why not?

Chapter Twenty-Two

What Hand to Play

*T**HE NEXT EVENING, YELLOW,** blue, and green 3x5 index cards were spread across Miranda's oak wood dining room table. She had placed three green index cards with the names of the men who had been murdered across the top of her table. Each had notes where their bodies were found and if they had tattoos.

With the extension added, the table provided ample room to spread out the cards and organize the names of the people murdered and anyone connected with them.

She had stopped at an office supply store on the way home to buy them, then another stop for enough Chinese food to feed her and Bryan for a week. The food, paper plates, and more were set on the kitchen counter, a bottle of wine included.

"Everything looks perfect, dear. Your young man should be very impressed."

"It's about time we're getting something done!"

"Precisely, Raymond. I agree," added Sherlock.

By the time he arrived a little after 8 p.m., her card system was beginning to take shape. Giving her a hello kiss on the cheek and looking at them, he hugged her like she did her father the night before. "Great idea. Food first, I'm starving."

While they sat at the counter to eat, she told him about seeing her father the night before. "I didn't know I was going to see him. It was as much a surprise to me as it is to you. Jacob left a note on my car for me to meet him. Then we went to see my father. Don't ask any questions until I finish. Please, Bryan, I'll tell you what they told me."

Bryan nodded his head yes.

Miranda repeated what she had been told. "Years ago, there was a successful international business syndicate. People all over the country and even a few overseas were members. It made millions of dollars through various illegal activities. Everyone who became a member had to get a tattoo of an elaborate circle on their upper left arm so they could identify each other. Jacob and Fish were members but decided the syndicate was heading in a very distasteful direction, which included drugs being sold to young people, so they had their tatoos removed. My father was never a member. They left him alone, and he kept his bookie and gambling business. He figured it was small time and no problem for them."

"Except it was," said Bryan.

"You promised."

"You're right. I'm sorry."

"Well, you're right," Miranda continued. "My father, with Jacob and Fish, came up with an idea for a gambling plan, ultimately bringing in millions of dollars. It included betting and gambling games amongst very wealthy people who were willing to bet on anything and everything. Believe me, I have no idea how it all worked. But apparently it did, and it worked very well."

"What happened?"

Miranda covered her face with her hands for a moment. "I promise, I'll tell you what I know. My father told me the syndicate became very upset when they realized how much money his plan, or I guess you could even call it a scheme, was making. Eventually they agreed on an arrangement where a percentage was given to the syndicate. However, apparently there was very bad blood between some of the original members and they blamed big losses they were experiencing on what my father was doing when, in fact, it was their own greed and infighting."

"Is that why he's disappeared this past year?" Bryan was trying to be both a detective and Miranda's friend... a close friend, he hoped.

"He said it had to do with it but not in the way you or I would think. He thinks the biggest problem is some of the children of those people are now very angry and vindictive and being pushed into being that way by a couple of the old timers."

"Meaning the murders."

Sighing and looking at him, "Yes. Jacob is sure they want to get to him and my father by threatening and hurting me."

"I'm sorry. I know I'm interrupting again, but I need to ask... what about the people in Madrid?"

"They're previous members of the syndicate. My father knew them and said they had started their own illegal operation. Once the murders at the zoo happened and they heard me talking about how familiar the tattoos were to me, it worried them. They figured the members' off-spring would want to hurt them too. My father said he went to warn them hours before the house blew up. And, yes, they bombed it themselves. Seems they've now headed for Brazil or some such place."

"Where is your father hiding? And, other than Jacob, who is helping him? I really need to know Miranda," Bryan after all was a detective.

"I don't know, Bryan. They wouldn't tell me. I *was* to

tell you they didn't commit any murders and to watch for people coming here from upstate New York. Oh, and by the way, Karla Ferrell is really Karla Frankel. Her father was one of the original members of the syndicate who died broke seven months ago."

"She's also disappeared. And by the way, did you ask him if he knows where your mother is?"

"No. I'm sure he could care even less than I do. She'll show up again someday, probably with another young guy in tow."

"Miranda, we need to figure out how to protect you until all this is solved. I've asked my captain for some extra help and also not to tell Wilson. He's been behaving very strange since these murders began."

Bryan picked up his glass of wine and went over to the table by the colored cards. As he was looking at them ready to make a few suggestions, Miranda told Bryan about the recent voices in her head.

"Don't laugh, but I keep hearing a suggestion to look beyond what you can see, and there's usually something else behind it."

Bryan didn't laugh. He knew it was really her good instincts.

"The green cards identify people who were murdered. The yellow cards are for potential murder suspects and any east coast visitors that can be identified," explained Miranda.

"And the blue ones? asked Bryan.

"They are for everyone in New Mexico connected to any of these people and each other."

"This won't be an easy task. You're going to need some additional cards," offered Agatha.

Sherlock added, *"Be aware that murders and murder suspects are bound to change."*

And watch out who you trust with all this stuff." Raymond always just told it like it was, with no frills attached.

One thing was certain. There were some long nights ahead for them all.

Chapter Twenty-Three

Seeking Revenge

THE ALBUQUERQUE POLICE WEREN'T aware of their arrival. They had been very clever. They drove west on what was once Rt. 66 in an older model Ford Toyota and made it a point to stay under the radar— no flashy car, no flashy clothes, no flashy wads of money. They had a credit card under a false name and false credentials, along with false licenses and car registration, even false passports. Just in case.

The two men arrived in Albuquerque days before the Madrid explosion. They rented an inexpensive furnished apartment at the edge of the south valley. It was the kind of place where the manager asked no questions. Within a few days of their arrival, they met up with Karla Frankel. The other man was now under arrest for the attempted kidnapping of Dr. Scott.

The two new visitors were from Queens, New York, the same as the ones who had arrived in Albuquerque almost four months ago. All were children of men who were members of the now defunct business syndicate. All four had a tattoo on their left arm like their fathers.

They were driven by the lies they had been told. They were the adult children of men who had great success with an illegal business syndicate for many years and then lost everything because they believed they could never be caught. But they were caught. Some were still in jail living out a life sentence.

Several of the men blamed Leonard and Jacob and their associates for their failures, leaving their families with a legacy of hate and, ultimately, revenge.

One of the newly arrived men was Jaxon (Jax) Powell, a forty-eight-year-old, short, stocky, mean, abusive man, who considered himself leader of this vengeful group. With him was his younger brother by four years, Peter, who did whatever Jax told him to do.

Karla Frankel, although considerably younger in her early thirties, had first met Jax when he came to meet with her father several months before. He was a charmer and a liar. It didn't take long for him to recruit her for his plans.

"Of course, I love you." He lied so easily.

"Once we get even with these people and get the money from them, we can get married." Jax put his arm around Karla, kissing her cheek, then her neck and downward.

Their plans to get that money were about blackmail and threats.

Like too many lonely women, Karla was willing to believe Jax and do whatever he asked her to do. When he told her to go to New Mexico for him she, of course, said yes. When he told her what he wanted her to do, she was hesitant but knew she couldn't say no to him.

"You're just using her," Peter told his brother.

"So what? As long as we get even with those people and get money from them, I'll use whoever I can." Jax finished a beer and got up for another one.

Months before he and his brother would drive west, he told Karla, "Listen to me, I want you to find a way to meet George Perez, then have him help you get a job at the zoo. He's head of security there. Understand?"

"How will I get there? And I'll need money to live." Karla was scared but more scared of making Jax angry. She knew he had a nasty temper. "I'll give you money, an airline ticket, and a resume to get the job." There were more kisses. Oh, he was very smooth. "Once you get the job, I'll tell you what to do next." The same person who set up his false information did the same for Karla. The night before she was to leave his final instructions were, "Here's a burner cell phone. Don't call me on anything else and only call if you really need to."

"When are you and Peter coming?" she asked. When she took his hand, he could feel how cold from fear she was. He didn't care one bit and with one of his delightful moves, patted her on the rear end.

"Once you have a job at the zoo, let me know. The sooner you get it, the sooner I can be there with you."

***

The other man, who arrived in Albuquerque before Jax, contacted Karla after she had been working at the zoo for a few months. A relative of Jax's, he told her, "Jax wants us to kidnap the zoo vet Miranda Scott and take her to your place. You'll need to know how to get us inside the zoo without alarms going off."

"What if they catch us? We'll be in big trouble." Karla sensed it was a very bad idea.

"No one will catch us. I know what I'm doing," he told her. Famous last words!

"Karla, Jax said to put your hair up and wear a base-ball cap. Also, you need to hire a couple teenage boys to toss candy laced with a heavy dose of pot to the animals to distract people from the kidnapping. Tell them the zoo is doing a test program. There are plenty of kids hanging out at nearby parks and school. Offer them $50 each. I'll drop off the candy and money at your apartment."

Karla, near tears, kept saying, "Ok. Sure, ok."

Then she called Jax sobbing.

"Do what he's telling you. Don't worry babe, I'll be there soon."

It was amazing how he could lie without any sense of guilt or concern for her. Everything planned and taking place was being carefully orchestrated.

Of the four involved, only Jax knew the strings of these criminal activities were being pulled by someone much higher up, by someone with a much greater need for revenge.

But Jax? He was driven by the possibility of the money promised him... by someone who was a far greater liar than he was.

Chapter Twenty-Four

Lineup

*I*T *WAS BUSY AT* the zoo. New animals had been brought to them requiring complete medical check-ups and quarantine time. There was an extra careful watch on the lioness after the dead body incident and discovering she was pregnant. And under beautiful, clear skies and warm days many children were brought to the zoo on field trips. On the weekends, families wandered through the grounds pointing at the animals, smiling, happy.

At the end of many days, Miranda and George went to watch Kamali herself. Her growing belly made them smile. He liked to join her there before locking up and making extra-sure everything was safe and secure.

"I still don't know how anyone got in here after dark," he told her.

"It's okay, the police are working on it." Miranda hugged him. She refused to believe he was in any way involved with the murders at the zoo.

***

Anderson arrived at Miranda's house right before sunset with treats for the dogs, another bottle of wine, and a kiss on the cheek and suggested, "It's possible there could be two murderers. The first two are very different from the hit on Dennis, or what has been set up to look like a hit."

Miranda wrote the names of people connected to anyone murdered or where they took place. The zoo. The senator's car.

He found himself staring at her.

She knew he was.

"Really, what are you waiting for? Kiss him." Raymond was insisting, *"Come on, kiss the guy!"*

Miranda went over to Bryan, put her arms around him, and kissed him long enough to make him want to toss the cards aside.

"There. Now we can get back to these cards." Miranda grinned.

Bryan was too surprised, and delighted, to say anything.

They set the blue index cards in a row below the green ones. Senator Graham, Carl Reed, Lillian Scott, Emma Parker, George Perez, and miscellaneous zoo staff who were connected in some way but not considered suspects.

At least not yet. After all anything is possible in solving a murder. Anyone could be the murderer.

There certainly were plenty of suspects.

"We need to include Jacob, Fish, and your father," Anderson insisted.

Miranda objected, "You're wrong." Reluctantly, she agreed to write each of their names on a blue card.

"Now dear, he is only doing his job." Agatha gently reminded her. *"He'll come around soon enough."*

"Reed and Graham could also be on this list, but we'll leave them off for now. Add yellow cards for the three people missing from the house in Madrid, Karla (Ferrell) Frankel, the alleged kidnapper, and write one with a question mark for whoever hired them."

Anderson looked at the cards spread out and then wrote "Detective Wilson" on a blue one.

"Really?" Miranda turned to look at him.

"He's been very cozy with the senator, which means a connection to Reed, and he found the dead body in the senator's car. Too many coincidences for my comfort."

"Does he know you're concerned about him?"

"I'm sure he senses I'm uncomfortable with his behavior. He's a darn good detective, but lately he's been different and I'm not sure why."

"You need to trust a partner," Miranda took his hand.

Reaching over and kissing her cheek, "How about a break?"

"*Well, aren't you two just the cutest.*" Raymond was such a wiseass.

"Sure. We can get something to eat at Maxim's bar. I'm starved." Miranda grabbed her jacket and keys and waved to the officer in the police car out front.

Anderson went over to him. "We'll be back in an hour. We're going to Maxim's bar not far from here. Make sure no one tries to break into the house."

It was one of those New Mexico nights when stars were spread across the sky and the evening air had cooled. The warmest days would become bearable, thanks to cooling and pleasant evenings. Bryan put his arm around Miranda as they walked and was pleased she didn't move it away. In the bar, each had a beer and burger.

Anderson's phone rang twice with calls from Wilson. He ignored them.

"*This is more than a bad feeling he has about Detective Wilson.*" Sherlock was always glad to offer an opinion.

"*I think he's protecting you.*" Agatha was always glad to offer an opinion too.

Enjoying the friendly neighborhood bar where many

people knew each other, they agreed to talk about anything but murder. Both of them laughed when an older man with grey hair in a ponytail and dressed in leopard pants and a bright yellow t-shirt walked in after they did and sat at the bar.

On the way out, Bryan patted him on the back, "Love your outfit."

Bryan recognized the man when he turned and said, "Groovy, thanks man."

Miranda smiled and walked out not giving it another thought. Detective Anderson did.

The groovy man was a police officer. Bryan guessed the captain was more concerned than he let on and sent him to keep an eye on him and Miranda. Apparently, the officer parked in front of Miranda's house had told the captain where they were going.

A wise precaution.

As they walked back to Miranda's house, a car slowly drove past them.

Shots were fired.

"Now what?" the voices in Miranda's head shouted.

Chapter Twenty-Five

Karla Frankel

*T*HE SHOTS MISSED THEM. They were clearly meant as a warning.

Driving past Miranda's house, the driver slowed once again. Someone opened the back door of the car and threw Karla Frankel's body on the street. The officer parked out front of Miranda's heard the shots and saw the body tossed out of the car. He called for backup, bringing more police and an ambulance.

Bryan and Miranda were fine

Karla Frankel didn't need an ambulance. She had been shot in the head. She needed a coroner.

An hour later, the car was found abandoned on a dead-end street by the undercover officer who had been in the bar. It had been reported stolen earlier in the day. Forensics would be kept busy with it for hours. There was blood in the trunk and back seat. There were fingerprints from half a dozen people.

"There are more bad guys in your life than a British Mystery," Agatha said.

"You mean more bad guys than in my stories," said Raymond, bragging.

Ignoring his colleagues, Sherlock announced, *"I believe things will escalate going forward. Mark my words."*

Miranda longed to tell them to shut up. There were too many people around for it to look like she was talking to herself.

***

The police were searching Karla's apartment for the second time. She had abandoned it after being implicated in the attempt to kidnap Miranda. Ramon Sanchez was the investigating officer. Wilson was clearly sidelined.

"Detective Anderson the place is a mess. It doesn't look like she's been back here."

"Talk to the neighbors. Maybe someone heard or saw something."

"I tried sir. Most people wouldn't open their door. It's easy to see they're afraid of getting involved. I'm going to take another look in the victim's apartment. When I was in there I thought there was a strong perfume smell. Seemed out of place."

"Karla might have gone there to hide something," said Anderson, who was appreciating working with this police officer. He had none of the bravado and obnoxious language which usually accompanied Detective Wilson.

Officer Sanchez had been on the force for almost ten years. He had been taught the importance of fairness and justice for everyone. His father and grandfather had been police officers where he grew up in Las Cruces, New Mexico. A little less than four hours from Albuquerque, it had become known in recent years as a travel destination, offering beautiful views along with great New Mexican culture and food. But when Sanchez was offered a job on the force in Albuquerque, he was thrilled to work and live, "in the big city."

In his late thirties, married with three kids, he had joined the force after two tours with the Marines. Everyone except the captain called him Ray and Detective Bryan Anderson found he liked working with him.

Sanchez had come back on the line. "Detective, I found something hidden under loose carpeting between the bedroom and bathroom. I'll meet you at the station with it."

Sanchez's find proved invaluable to the investigation of Karla Frankel's murder and even offered a clue to the other murders. Brian asked himself how he could replace Wilson with Sanchez. He then burst out laughing and got some strange looks from others in the police station. He realized now he was hearing voices in *his* head!

He knew an opportunity would present itself soon enough thinking how Wilson was clearly on the road to self-destruction.

***

"Bryan, honest I'm fine," Miranda told him when he called to check on her. Like every half hour! "The doors are locked, the dogs are inside, and a police officer is now parked in my driveway. Soon you'll have one sleeping on my sofa."

"Only me, sweetheart."

"Don't get mad, I'm going to call Jacob. I'll feel better if he knows what's happening."

Bryan didn't argue. "I'll stop over later."

***

At police headquarters, Sanchez started to hand over the evidence bag from Karla's apartment to Detective Anderson. Wilson, standing near them, tried to grab it away. Anderson pulled it back, "You're not on this case anymore, Tom. If you have a problem, better go talk to the captain."

"What the hell...? Bull!" Wilson stopped. He didn't want to get in trouble with the captain. He didn't want to risk being investigated. He turned and stormed out of the room and out of the building. Quickly making a call, he shouted into the phone, "We need to meet! Now!"

The captain saw him rush out of the building and watched him from his window until a car picked him up. Wilson was getting more and more careless... and desperate.

After the drama with Wilson, Anderson put on gloves and took the evidence carefully out of the bag Sanchez handed him. "It's an airline ticket to La Guardia airport. She was planning on leaving tonight. But see what's attached. It was a one-way ticket and boarding pass for her trip here."

"Ray this could be the lead we've been needing. Nice work." He noticed that Wilson had left headquarters without talking to the captain.

Anderson put the tickets back in the evidence bag. "Contact the airline she arrived on and find out who paid for her tickets. I'll give these to forensics to see if they can find any fingerprints on them other than Karla's."

"Sir, I'll have the airports check their cameras for the day she left back east and when she arrived here. Maybe someone was with her one of those times."

Anderson was impressed with the officer and told him, "You would make a good detective one day."

"I think I might like that," he replied with a smile.

"Call me if you find out anything," said Anderson. He stopped to tell the captain what was happening and asked if he wanted to discuss Wilson. The captain's one word answer, "later," said a lot.

He was on his way to check on Miranda and knew "later" would be coming soon enough. Wilson had seemingly crossed over to the dark side.

She was staring at the index cards on the table, her

dogs sitting close by, when Bryan knocked on the door. Miranda let him in and he threw his jacket on a chair. "Any wine left?" He sounded exhausted and frustrated.

Miranda poured some wine for the two of them and asked, "Do you know anything yet about Karla's murder?" "The car was found abandoned. Of course, it was stolen. We're working on some other leads."

"*I deduct that he knows more than he says,*" Sherlock said smugly.

"*Stop being such a know it all,*" Raymond responded.

"*He is just trying to protect her,*" Agatha sweetly commented.

"*That may be the case, but I still think he's on to something,*" said Sherlock sounding very positive.

"Anything you want to share?" Miranda took a green card and wrote Karla (Ferrell) Frankel on it. She would eventually add where she was killed and that she had a familiar tattoo on her left arm. She and Bryan had seen it when the body was lying on the street in front of her house.

"Later, when we have more details. I think someone is masterminding everything happening here. I'm sure of it. Only I don't know if they're here or back east."

"How can you find out?" Miranda had a bad feeling what he was about to ask.

"I want to meet with Jacob and Fish... and your father. I promise no one else will know. I'm sure they understood how those who ran the syndicate worked. It was its own unique world of mobsters with their own rules and they didn't believe rules for others applied to them."

She knew he was right and silently shook her head yes to setting up a meeting with the other men in her life.

Chapter Twenty-Six

The Meeting

TWO NIGHTS LATER A little after 10 p.m., Bryan and Miranda drove to the meeting he had requested. Jacob and Fish were driving behind them to be sure they weren't being followed. The Corrales restaurant was opened only for the private meeting as a personal favor to Jacob.

The local streets were dark and quiet. The shops and restaurants in the small village were closed. They drove past several art galleries, the library, and a few homes with lights on, noticing the air smelled fresher away from city traffic. Miranda's father opened the door to let them in. First, she hugged him, then introduced him to Bryan.

A round table in the back was set up with five glasses and a bottle of wine. Miranda sat down between her father and Jacob.

"Just let them talk," said Raymond, giving his professional opinion.

"Only if they offer facts and not stories," Sherlock declared.

Jacob took her hand, leaned over, and whispered, "You like him, don't you?"

She pulled her hand away and poured herself a very large glass of wine. Even though she had agreed with Bryan this meeting could provide information helpful in finding the people committing these murders and intent on harming her, it was still uncomfortable. These men were family! Yes, even Fish felt like family. The voice in her head agreed.

"Now dear, you know you can trust everyone here," said Agatha.

Anderson rested his elbows on the table and folded his hands. "Thank you for agreeing to meet. You have my word no one else will know about it and no one will know where I got any information you might provide tonight. Here's what I need to know. How are the people from the defunct east coast business syndicate involved in the murders at the zoo and attempts to harm Miranda? Who is in charge of what is happening?" Anderson sat back, poured himself some wine and let the men talk.

Jacob began, "I was a member of the syndicate for about three years, so was Fish. Leonard wisely wanted no part of it. There were about two dozen families involved and everyone was making a lot of money through several illegal activities. Members needed to get a tattoo on their upper left arm so they could be identified as a part of the syndicate."

"Did you have a problem with them when you wanted to leave the syndicate?" Anderson asked.

"No. Not at all. It left more money for those still involved. We were asked—well, more like told—to have our tattoos removed, which was fine with me and Fish."

The owner of the restaurant, who had been up front organizing the bar suddenly came back. "Sorry. Someone is knocking at the door. Give me a minute and I'll get rid of them."

It was a few moments of quiet anxiety until he came back grinning. "It was only a local drunk wanting a drink.

He saw the car parked outside and thought we were open. I said it was a private family gathering and sent him off."

It reminded all of them how much fear and concern the zoo murders had brought into their lives. At this point everyone drank some wine.

Leonard Scott set his glass down. "I had an idea for an international betting operation, and Jacob and Fish joined me when they left the syndicate. Another half dozen people got involved and its success grew beyond anything we imagined possible."

"Is this some of what I saw you and other men doing in our home?" Miranda wanted to know.

"Let it go dear. It was a long time ago," said Agatha wisely.

"Yes. However, I assure you the three of us here have not been involved in anything like that for many years." Leonard looked at the detective. "Really, we haven't!"

"So why the problem and why now? Some people are clearly intent on making big trouble for you and attempting to get to you by threatening Miranda."

Jacob stood up, "I'm getting us another bottle of wine. We have a way to go."

"I'll get it. You two need to tell him why they're seeking revenge." Fish walked up front to get the wine.

Jacob stood up to stretch. "He's right, of course. Fish doesn't talk much but he can be very wise at times. I'll start, then Leonard can tell you the rest."

Fish came back with a second bottle of wine and tray of appetizers the owner had prepared. "He says he's leaving, and Jacob knows how to lock up and put on the alarm."

Jacob nodded okay and began to explain. "We were making so much money while they were losing millions, getting indicted for illegal activities, sentenced to prison, and ultimately leaving their families struggling. Those who started the syndicate are now old, and some died in jail. However, one family continued telling lies about what happened, saying we were to blame."

"Did you ever meet with them, try to get them to stop?" Miranda interrupted him.

"Yes. The head of the family refused. I think getting older and restless has stirred up that anger and resentment. More like an excuse for him. Even though he's old and getting senile, he's still head of the family. It's best if Leonard tells you the rest."

Miranda thought her father look tired. She always thought of him as youthful and energetic. Even exciting. Not tonight. He was clearly weary.

"The head of the syndicate's founding family has been telling his children and their friends it was Jacob and I who caused them their problems and put them out of business. We got word from someone back east that he is expecting, actually *demanding*, his children seek revenge and get money from us. It's absurd. He even insisted they get the syndicate tattoos." Leonard paused.

"Have they tried to contact you, blackmail, or threaten you?" Anderson waited for an answer while Miranda looked at her father.

"Indirectly, yes. They are demanding millions of dollars. We refused." Leonard sighed. "The first two bodies were found at the zoo after that. Seems those two men changed their minds about being involved in their plans for revenge. I'm not sure why Karla Frankel was killed. You'll have to figure out that one."

"I'm so sorry sweetheart," her father continued. "Detective, these people are murderers and they're trying to hurt my daughter unless we give them what they want. For one thing, we don't have the kind of money they're asking for."

Anderson stood up to stretch and reached over for some food.

Leonard took the moment to ask, "So, what about you two?"

"What about us?" Miranda gently punched her father in the arm.

"*It is apparent—even to your father—that you are fond of this young detective,*" said Sherlock.

"*Let's get back to the story,*" urged Raymond.

Detective Anderson grinned. "What did the people in Madrid have to do with all of this?"

"Truly, absolutely nothing. They wanted to run an operation like we had years ago and remembered Madrid as a quiet place to set it up. The people back east thought they were connected to Jacob and me, and that we were all getting ready to make a lot of money again. So did Miranda's friend Dennis—thanks to Lillian, my not-so-charming ex-wife. I heard about it—never mind how—and went there to warn them. They had been anxious when they heard Miranda talking about the men murdered at the zoo having tattoos. That's why they wanted to meet with her, to get her to stop talking about them. The three people in the house in Madrid knew the people from the syndicate and how vindictive and violent they could be." Leonard Scott got up, pacing, and then leaned over to Jacob to whisper something.

"Is that why they blew up their house and fled the country?" asked Bryan. Leonard and Jacob both nodded yes.

"Do you know what happened to the dog they had in their back yard?" Miranda interrupted, and they all looked at her. It mattered to her!

"I do," answered Fish. "I was there the day before they planned to destroy the house and I took it to a shelter."

Bryan broke in. "I need to know who is running this revenge game. Are they here or back east? What are the names of the children of the men who began the syndicate?"

It would take almost another hour to get most of the information he asked for, before he shook their hands and thanked them. He was sure he didn't have all the children's names. Certainly, some had their names changed when they were married.

"We aren't sure who is in charge here in Albuquerque," Jacob added.

Anderson had two more questions, "Do you think these people killed Dennis Huxley, and do you know where Lillian Scott is?"

"No to both questions. Don't care." Leonard answered shrugging his shoulders and getting up to leave.

Then he took his daughter aside and gave her a hug. "I noticed the looks between you two, sweetheart. He seems like a good man."

"I like your father. Even if he used to be a gangster." Sherlock was never one to mince words.

She was concerned it was possible this would be the last time she would see these three men for a long time... if ever.

What if they were murdered?

Chapter Twenty-Seven

The Trouble with Wilson

"**W**_HERE THE HELL ARE_ you, and why aren't you answering my calls? I'm your partner, damn it!" Detective Thomas Wilson was in a panic. Anderson told him he was off the zoo murders case and should talk to the captain... something he was avoiding.

The morning after his meeting in Corrales Anderson closed the door to the captain's office and, sitting across from him in a room filled with family photos and personal decorations, told him both a little and a lot. "I have information from a confidential source about a defunct syndicate back east stirring up revenge. Sir, I'm sure it's connected to the zoo murders and more."

"Reliable?" The captain asked.

"Very. And if possible I'd like to have officer Sanchez assigned to work with me full time. There's a lot of trouble with Wilson. I can't trust him anymore."

"You think this stuff with Wilson is serious?" The captain looked at him as he buzzed for Sanchez to come into his office.

"I do." Anderson sighed, knowing he had just sealed Wilson's fate as a police detective.

After informing Sanchez he would be working with

Anderson, the captain said, "Tell him what's happening and what you need. I'm going to take care of the other matter."

Anderson updated him then told him, "Meet me at Miranda Scott's house about 7 p.m. I have something to show you."

Sanchez smiled, "Thanks. Just text me her address."

Anderson told her about Sanchez coming too.

***

Two police officers found Wilson at home and brought him to the station. The captain signaled for Anderson to join them. Wilson's eyes were bloodshot, his clothes rumpled, and he was acting jittery. He seemed paranoid. Or, was it guilt?

"I want a lawyer," he demanded when he saw Anderson. "You're just out to burn me because I'm better at my job than you! You're jealous because I'm friendly with the senator."

"Detective, no one's accused you of anything." The captain told him.

Wilson quieted and looked at Anderson as if he was pleading for help or understanding.

"Tom, what lawyer should we call? Meantime, how about you stay in the station's conference room until your lawyer gets here."

Wilson was calmer as Anderson walked him to the conference room. He handed an officer a business card with the name of a law firm to call. "Tell them it's important."

Quietly Anderson told the officer, "Stand by the door. Don't let him leave the building."

Two hours later an attorney handed her card to a police officer who took her to Wilson. She was from the same law firm who represented the senator. Of course.

In less than a half hour, she got up and went to speak with the captain. Wilson was allowed to leave with the attorney's guarantee they would be back Monday to answer questions and make a statement. He was not a client she particularly wanted. She actually told him as much!

"I'm here as a favor to the senator."

Truth was, the senator didn't want Wilson blabbing about their relationship. He knew too much.

Anderson had a list of questions for Wilson, especially regarding the senator and Reed. There was still the strange unsolved murder of Dennis Huxley and Wilson finding his body. He was sure Wilson knew what happened.

They would have to wait until Monday. It didn't feel like the best idea to Bryan Anderson.

Meantime, he was anxious to show Sanchez the index cards and update him on what he knew about the case.

From 7 p.m. to a little after 9, Miranda, Bryan, and Ray discussed the case and formed ideas for moving forward. The information from the meeting in Corrales provided a broader picture. Sanchez accepted, without comment, it had come from a confidential source.

"Miranda, I need to review a copy of Karla Frankel's zoo job application and resume. And might as well get me one for George Perez." Bryan then turned to Sanchez.

"I'm hoping you're good on the computer. See how many more names of members of the business syndicate and their family members you can get. I'll be doing some checking on Detective Wilson. He's coming into the station with his attorney after the weekend. I really have a bad feeling about him and the senator."

Miranda had grown up in a world surrounded by illegal activities and was only beginning to realize its impact on her. Her lack of trust and being cautious about having a romantic relationship with Bryan certainly stemmed partly from that experience.

"*I thought Wilson was a bad egg,*" said Raymond.

"*His actions prove you're quite right,*" agreed Sherlock.

Chapter Twenty-Eight

Open House

*A*S IF BEING CONNECTED to several murders and being involved with the investigations (informally, of course) wasn't enough to keep Miranda up nights, Emma decided to plan an Open House Weekend at the Zoo to promote the baby naming contest.

"It should help our image after the negative publicity from the murders," she told Miranda in hopes of getting her enthused about it.

"I don't feel great about doing this. Do you really think it's wise after all that's been happening?" Miranda was bothered by Emma insisting on doing it now.

"Trust your instincts," said Raymond, tough and smart as always.

Emma was determined! "Yes. We don't want people to be afraid to come here. It will help to offer a weekend of fun with free stuff and the final chance to enter the contest to name the baby zebra."

Deidre Carter, who had been managing the media for the zoo through the murders, was glad to finally have a reason to send an upbeat press announcement to the local news.

George Perez, concerned about big crowds, told Emma and Miranda, "We'll need extra security."

"I agree," said Miranda.

Emma got her way.

The Albuquerque weather cooperated with two beautiful days of clear blue skies and little wind. Wind often complicated events in the city, especially the week of the annual balloon fiesta. There was no entry fee and children twelve and under were given gift bags which included a family pass for another visit.

George walked the grounds each day, checking with the other guards and making sure everything was running smoothly.

No one knew they were there.

Jax and his brother Peter visited the zoo. They took a city bus there and mingled with the hundreds of others who attended each day. No one would know until after the weekend they had been there.

Before leaving, they filled out a baby naming form and dropped it in the large bin designed to look like a zebra. They felt safe since no one knew what they looked like.

"Thank goodness this weekend is over," said Bryan. He and Sanchez (who insisted they call him Ray) were back at Miranda's house Monday evening. She gave Bryan the copies of the resumes and job applications he had asked for.

Ray gave him an update regarding the names of the syndicate family's children. "I should have a full list for you by the end of the week. A couple of the computer geeks at the station are helping with the search."

"What does Karla's resume say? I'm sure it's probably all false." Bryan was reaching for his phone ringing in his coat pocket.

"Damn it! Both days? Bring those forms to the police station and we'll meet you there." He was furious.

Miranda reached over to take his hand but he pulled

it away, and getting up to leave shouted, "The murderers showed up at your zoo's damn event!"

"What?" Ray stood up to go with him.

"George Perez was sorting through the baby naming forms. The murderers filled out a form each day and put them in the barrel. 'Sorry you missed us, the *Zoo Murderers*.' 'We're here again, love all, the *Zoo Murderers*.' Now they're taunting us. Damn them and damn the whole Zoo Open House weekend!" Detective Anderson rarely showed this much anger.

Miranda knew there was nothing she could say. And she knew she had been right about not wanting to have this event.

Ray tried. "Sir, there could be fingerprints or some DNA on them."

"Call forensics to meet us at the station, I'll tell Perez to bring those forms to us."

As Ray made the call, Bryan turned around and went over to Miranda and gave her a kiss on the cheek. "Sorry, I know the Zoo Open House wasn't your idea."

***

Monday morning came and went, and Thomas Wilson did not show up at the police station.

No one knew where he was. Not even his attorney.

Chapter Twenty-Nine

The Fate of Vengeance

JAX AND HIS BROTHER were living in a cramped small apartment and running out of money. All their plans had failed so far. Now Jax had to call the person heading this operation for advice. He was dreading it.

They had their bit of fun at the zoo. They thought they were clever, taunting and evading authorities.

Karla was dead. The other attempted kidnapper was under arrest. Jax and Peter were cocky and confident, even after the person back east blasted them for their problems and mishaps. "I want drastic action immediately!" the man shouted along with a string of curse words.

Jax hung up furious, "Like what we've done so far hasn't been drastic! He said we should expect someone here to be in touch with us the next few days. He wouldn't say who it is. Oh, and we're not to do anything until we hear from them. Bull. The guy is old and senile. To hell with him! I have ideas of my own. Once we get the money, we won't have to share it with him or anyone else."

When the old man back east hung up, he shouted even louder, "Damn stupid fools!" to a frightened older woman.

Of course, Jax didn't know the police had found fingerprints on the airline tickets Karla had hidden in her apartment matching the ones on the zoo contest forms.

Jaxson Powell's name lit up on the computer showing a long police record.

Ray showed Anderson and the captain Jaxson's mug shot taken three years ago in Queens, when he was arrested for robbing a jewelry store and beating up the owner. "He got probation thanks to some hot shot, well-connected lawyer. Before his stint as a jewelry thief, he was arrested for stealing cars and beating up a girlfriend. Surprisingly, he was never arrested for anything to do with drugs. He usually runs with his younger brother, Peter, whose record is peppered with less violent offences. It seems his big brother's lawyer has also managed to keep baby brother out of the spotlight."

Anderson liked working with Officer Sanchez more and more. "Let's get his photo out to the media and police throughout the state. I'm going to the zoo. I want to show his photo to Perez. Maybe he remembers seeing him there. Maybe Emma and Miranda will recognize him."

The captain complimented them, "Good work. By the way, it's Tuesday afternoon and there's still no sign of Wilson. I'll give his attorney one more day to get him here."

***

Bryan realized things were getting complicated between him and Miranda. His feelings for her were stronger than ever, as well as his concern for her safety. He still wasn't sure though if her father and Jacob were involved in this mess somehow. It was a huge concern at this point in their relationship.

"Great, I've fallen in love with a gangster's daughter," he said aloud to himself. He called Miranda and said, "I'll be there shortly. Tell Emma and George I need to meet with all of you. "I have a photo I want you to look at."

"Something is finally changing in this case," said Sherlock.

"It's about time, isn't it?" There was always impatience and sarcasm from Raymond.

Emma, Miranda, and Perez looked at the photo but none of them recalled seeing the person in the picture at the zoo. Perez agreed to show the photo to the other security guards. "I'll check our security camera footage as well."

Miranda walked with Bryan to the parking lot, shaken the murderers had been at the zoo when so many people were there. "Do you and Ray want to continue tonight?"

"Just me. I'll fill you in later. It should be about 7. I'll bring food and wine. See how sweet I am?" Giving her an extra-long kiss on the cheek, he left and called Ray with an idea.

"What if we told the local news the murder of Karla Frankel has been solved? We can tell them we've found fingerprints on clothes she was wearing when she was shot. Have Deidre send the announcement out along with Karla's photo."

"Great idea. Want me to pass it by the captain?" Ray asked Anderson.

"Yeah. If he says yes, run with it. And thanks!"

It was almost 7:30 when Bryan knocked on Miranda's door carrying in Mexican food, a bottle of wine and dessert from a favorite local bakery. While they ate at her kitchen counter, the dogs under their feet waiting for treats, he told her about sending out an announcement to the media about Karla and her murderers.

"There's definitely connections with more people." Miranda suggested.

Bryan agreed, "Maybe once we get the names of the syndicate member's children, it will help to identify them."

"I made some changes to the index cards. I added a green card for Karla. We don't know exactly where she was murdered." Miranda had also written below the names of the murder victims, "Who else are they related to?"

On yellow cards for suspects, she added Jaxson Powell, Peter Powell, and the man in jail who had attempted to kidnap her. His attorney had no success in getting him out on bail.

Sanchez's research would show Karla was the youngest in a family of five children. She grew up with two older brothers and two older sisters. All four were married, although it was uncertain where a couple of them were living. It was a family with strong ties to the earliest members of the business syndicate.

Standing next to Miranda, Bryan moved Wilson's name to a yellow card. "I have to consider him for Dennis's murder. He was supposed to show up at the station with his attorney yesterday and we still don't know where he is. Captain is giving him another day and then we'll have to put out an arrest warrant for him."

"Doesn't he have a strong connection to the senator? Maybe he knows where he is?"

Bryan hugged her. "Of course! Even his attorney is from the firm representing the senator. You're brilliant."

"He really is quite fond of you in a sentimental sort of way," Sherlock commented.

"Oh behave, Sherlock. You never like sentiment," commented Agatha.

It was after 10 when he sent the email. "Senator, this is Detective Anderson. You and Reed need to be at the police station at noon tomorrow." He copied Sanchez and the captain on the email. They would know it related to Wilson.

Miranda and Bryan went out into her backyard and

waited while the dogs had their evening outing and play-time.

"When all this is over, we need to talk." Bryan put his arm around her.

"Really, about what?" Miranda raised her eyebrows and grinned, knowing full well what he meant.

"Don't be a hard to get along with dame," chided Ray-mond, forever difficult himself.

Bryan smiled. "Us." He put his arm around her, giving her much more than a casual kiss, then left for home. Lots of things were about to change.

Chapter Thirty

Brazen Behavior

SENATOR GRAHAM STRUTTED INTO the station shortly after noon. Two attorneys from his favorite law firm and Carl Reed followed behind him. His arrogance was visible. Anderson's patience with the Senator's nonsense was reaching its limit.

Putting them into the larger conference room, he left a police officer at the door telling him, "The senator and Reed are not to leave until I'm finished with them. The lawyers can stay or go, makes no difference to me."

The senator was making quite a scene, cursing about having to be there, until Detective Anderson went in. "Detective Thomas Wilson, an associate of yours, is missing. It would be helpful to your situation if you could let us know where he is."

The lawyer sitting next to the senator responded, "It's not clear what you mean by their situation, but I assure you these men know nothing as to the whereabouts of your Detective Wilson."

Anderson placed a phone log call sheet on the long rectangle table, "All the yellow highlighted calls are from Wilson to the senator and the ones highlighted in green are from him to Wilson. Looks like to me like they're pretty cozy with each other."

"Detective," the younger of the two attorneys responded, "Certainly they are in touch with each other. Detective Wilson has been very thoughtful in protecting Senator Graham and Mr. Reed."

"How nice of him," Anderson replied sarcastically.

Addressing the senator and Reed, Anderson said, "I want a direct answer. Do you know where we can find Detective Wilson?"

Both men shook their heads no. These were men comfortable with lying.

Anderson continued, "If Wilson isn't found by tomorrow, there will be an arrest warrant out for him and you can be sure we'll be going through his computers, phones, mail, and bank accounts."

The older attorney stood up, "Is my client under arrest?"

"Not at this time. But senator, you and Reed are not to leave town." Anderson was enjoying this!

***

As the interview with the senator was happening, Karla's photo was being shown on the news on all three local television stations, with the reporters reading the prepared police statement. The photos of the Powell brothers were also shown and they were noted as "persons of interest" in several murders.

Within the first half hour of it airing on the noon news, the station received over a dozen calls. Most were not reliable. Then an anonymous caller muffling his or her voice was very specific. "I've seen this guy. I saw him the past weekend walking around the zoo with another guy. I remember because both of them had what I thought was a strange tattoo on their arms."

The officer who had picked up the call waved Anderson to his desk. Anderson told the officer, "Ask them which day and what time they saw them?"

"I did. They said around 2 p.m. on the first day."

It bothered him the men would let their tattoos show. The call finished, Anderson contacted the zoo.

"Emma, it's Detective Anderson. I need to see the security footage from the first day of the Open House at the zoo from 1-3 p.m. I'll be over in half an hour. Ask George and Miranda to be there."

"Okay regarding George. Miranda's in surgery. I'll let her know when she's done." Emma hung up and buzzed George to be in her office and requested the security footage from the weekend event.

Before going to the zoo, Bryan texted Ray to tell him what was happening. "If you can, meet me at the zoo curator's office."

Later, in Emma's office, all four watched the footage. The film showed that on Saturday at 2:10 p.m., Jaxson and his brother stood by the zebra habitat filling out baby naming forms and that their tatoos were, in fact, visible. Miranda walked in as George told Officer Sanchez, "I'll get a copy of this to you by the end of the day."

They played the film again so Miranda could see it. "They certainly were brazen and apparently oblivious they could possibly be seen."

Anderson told Emma, "I want security increased until we catch these two."

Miranda started to walk out, then turned and asked Bryan, "Do you think these two committed the murders at the Zoo?"

"Yes."

Chapter Thirty-One

Schemes and Scams

THE CALL WOKE DETECTIVE Anderson at 6:30 a.m. "Detective Wilson has been found dead in his car in front of the police station. We were told to call you."

Now wide awake Bryan said, "I'll be right there."

"It appears to be suicide. It looks like he shot himself in the side of his head. There's also a large envelope here with your name on it. The coroner is on her way." The officer on the scene was doing his best to stay professional in spite of the awful mess.

"Don't move anything. Don't touch the envelope." Anderson was at the station in twenty minutes. Reporters and cameramen were already gathered around the station.

Anderson got two text messages on his way to the station, "I heard. I'll be there soon. Ray."

The other one, "I'm so sorry. Miranda." She had seen the Special Bulletin on the early morning news.

The scene inside Wilson's car was indeed a huge mess. Turning to Ray when he arrived, Anderson shook his head in disbelief. "I need an evidence bag for this envelope he left for me. Good grief, he blew his brains out. They're all over the inside of his car."

Crime scene tape and barriers had, of course, been

put up, keeping the media and stray onlookers away. The captain arrived telling Anderson and Ray, "You better come inside with me."

Ray handed Bryan the evidence bag. Once they got to the captain's office, Bryan opened the envelope. Inside was a letter from Detective Wilson, together with accounting books filled with information regarding illegal schemes to raise money for the senator.

The letter explained, "Only a small percentage of the money went to the senator's political campaigns over the past ten years, but the senator and Reed kept a significant amount. Payments were also made to me for helping the senator stay out of police trouble. He frequently beat up prostitutes after spending time with them."

The letter continued, "The senator told me Dennis (Hayes) Huxley was trying to blackmail him and had proof of his illegal activities, found in papers at the law firm where he worked. The senator asked me to get rid of him and make it look like Reed did it."

Bryan read the entire letter and then handed it to the captain, who passed it on to Ray. Near the end of the letter—in bold caps—Wilson had written, "I HAD NOTHING TO DO WITH THE MURDERS AT THE ZOO."

The senator made a statement to the media. "I'm profoundly sad for the city's loss of such a good detective." He, of course, had no idea of the legacy Wilson left.

For the next two days, Bryan, Ray, and other officers in the department were busy gathering evidence and preparing warrants for their case against Senor Graham and Reed.

"Anderson. You and Sanchez attend the funeral. After that, bring in those two S.O.B.s." The captain was determined to handle the situation the way he wanted. "Let them stew a bit, wondering if Wilson told us about their schemes and scams."

It was a private service, no police escort, procession, or tributes. The media department put out a brief announcement.

After Detective Wilson was laid to rest, the senator and Reed were once again brought in for more questioning.

They were told to be at the station at 10 a.m., the day after Wilson's funeral. The senator marched in, arrogant as ever, with Reed and two attorneys. The news media waited outside for the statement he promised them.

Detective Anderson started laughing, telling Ray and the captain, "I can't wait for the media to see him and his flunky in handcuffs. Now there's a great statement!"

This time they were brought into an interrogation room. Officer Sanchez turned on the tape recorder. One of the attorneys immediately started to announce his client's annoyance at being called to the station like a common criminal.

Anderson told him, "Be quiet please. We have a letter Detective Wilson left for us. You can make comments when we're finished reading it."

The senator pushed his chair back, face flushed, screaming, "I'm leaving. I refused to be harassed." Reed literally turned white. Two officers were standing at the door outside the interrogation room. The senator wasn't going anywhere. His lawyer whispered in his ear attempting to calm him down.

With the tape recorder on, Anderson started reading Wilson's statement.

Reed was rubbing his forehead as the detective read the letter beginning with the accusation of money laundering schemes, political kickbacks, and payoff's.

Then Anderson got to the end of the letter. "The senator told me Dennis Huxley was trying to blackmail him and had proof of his illegal activities found in papers at the law firm where he worked. Senator Graham asked me to get rid of him and make it look like Reed did it."

The senator, his face now a deep red, screamed again, "He's a damn liar! You can't believe anything he's telling you!"

Reed didn't hesitate to reach over and punch the senator, giving him a bloody nose and calling him a variety of obscene names. Sanchez pushed him back in his chair while the senator was trying to regain his composure.

"The letter is signed by Thomas Wilson," Anderson concluded as he stood up. "Senator Graham and Carl Reed, you're both under arrest. Officer Sanchez, please read these men their rights."

Graham went berserk. Reed remained oddly quiet. Anderson handed a copy of the letter to both lawyers.

The story of the senator's arrest was featured on every local television station and mentioned on some national news, as well. "True, he'll be out on bail, and maybe never do any jail time, but his career will certainly be over," Detective Anderson leaned back and sighed.

"The rich and powerful, even when they fall, all too often escape justice."

Senator Graham's story continued to be, "I'm innocent." His was an entirely unbelievable story.

***

Bryan was angry with Wilson for participating in illegal activities, and he was also sad. They had done a lot of good police work together for many years and, until the last couple of years, had been friends.

The past always holds memories, good and bad. Wilson was sadly now part of the past. True, his actions affected the future of others, but they would have to find their own answers. The senator and Reed were part of a future demanding accountability for their actions.

For now, there were still other problems needing Detective Anderson's attention. "Ray, I want to follow up on the responses regarding the two men seen at the zoo."

The television coverage of the Powell brothers had forced them into hiding and the news found its way back east. For the second time in one week, the head of the family in Queens spoke to Jax, this time acting very concerned, almost fatherly. "Be careful boys. Stay out of sight. Someone will call to help you get out of New Mexico." Click.

Then calling his contact in New Mexico, the old man—not senile at all—gave the execution order for the Powell brothers. "They're a big problem. Get rid of them."

***

Miranda left Jacob a message. "The police know the Powell brothers killed the two people at the zoo and Karla Frankel. Not you or my father. I hope I get to see you soon. Much love."

"What a relief! Still, why is her father hiding?" Sherlock was right.

It seemed to Miranda people she had been working with for many years were acting different. Perhaps, she was too. The past weeks had been very trying. Everyone had a story to explain the reasons for their behavior. Some told the truth. Others embellished their experiences. And still others lied—a lot and often.

Miranda usually had a good a sense when people were lying, maybe because she grew up with a mother who was a pro at it. So, who was lying now?

Raymond was wondering the same thing. *"Something doesn't feel right at the zoo."* He sounded skeptical of everyone.

"*I admit, I have to agree with you.*" Agatha sounded worried.

"*We need to look more closely at the zoo employees,*" added Sherlock.

Chapter Thirty-Two

Suspicious

*M*IRANDA COULDN'T SHAKE THE bad feeling she had about the zoo. Something wasn't right and kept nagging at her. Agatha, Raymond, and Sherlock were making sure she didn't.

George's story was simple. He was in love. "Sorry, I've been distracted. I met someone through my choir group. Stop laughing. Yes, I like to sing."

Emma's story was also simple. "With the murders happening here and now knowing the murderers were walking around the zoo, it's freaked me out some. I've been distracted and worried about the zoo and the animals."

"Everything will work out. Give it time," said Agatha, hoping to convince Miranda.

"Pay attention to what is happening around you," added Raymond.

Sherlock just shook his head in agreement.

The zoo kept everyone busy with animals who required medical checkups, the dietician changing some animals' diets, and the dozens of daily actions and people required to keep it running smoothly. And through it all, were the underlying fears of what might happen next.

They knew the Powell brothers were responsible for

the three murders. Anderson wasn't convinced they acted on their own. "I'm sure someone in New Mexico has been in charge of those two dimwits. Before they went completely off the grid, they left the note taped to your car window demanding money from your father."

It would be almost two weeks before the dimwits showed up, dehydrated and scared. They had been hiding in a deserted cabin in the mountains outside of Albuquerque. They, too, had quite a story.

Chapter Thirty-Three

Volunteers

A *LOCAL WOMAN WHO* would be 90 years old in a couple months won the zebra baby naming contest. It made for a great story with photos of the winner and baby Zebra now known as Luna, the Spanish word for moon. It was almost a full moon when she was born.

To celebrate that there was some good news, Emma and Miranda went out to dinner and were able to laugh at what they might be like when they were 90 years old.

"In a couple months, we'll be looking for a name for one or two lion cubs. No naming contest," Emma promised.

"Do you think we need to get a new vet intern? I'm concerned with the cubs due in a couple months and with several other zoo animals pregnant we're going to need more help," said Miranda. She was being very tactful in making the suggestion since Emma had been the one to hire Karla.

Emma smiled. "It's okay. Ferrell—or Frankel—was a bad hire for sure. But we actually have more than enough volunteers. We could train a couple of them to help you in the hospital and for medical care."

"Emma, it could work! Let me look through some of the volunteer applications and see if any of them have medical or healthcare experience of any kind. I don't want anyone passing out from the sight of blood."

"Like me." Emma laughed. "Okay, I'll give them to you tomorrow."

"*You need to talk to Bryan. Maybe he should check out the volunteers,*" said Agatha firmly.

"*Wow, I thought it was my role to be overly suspicious,*" laughed Raymond.

The women gave each other a goodnight hug, and went home their separate ways. Getting home, waving to the police officer out front, then letting out her dogs, Miranda called Bryan. "I need to see you, I have an idea."

"Hi sweetheart, I'd love to see you too, but it's almost midnight and I have an early morning. Can we get together tomorrow night?"

"Sorry. Yes. Bring Sanchez." Miranda hung up realizing she, too, was exhausted. She was also sure she had hit on something worth exploring.

***

There were ample amounts of delicious lasagna and salad from a local favorite Italian restaurant and, of course, red wine.

The two men walked in at almost the same time and noticed the pile of zoo folders on the table by the index cards.

While they were enjoying the food and wine, Miranda told them about her conversation with Emma. "We came up with the idea of using some volunteers to assist me instead of hiring another vet intern."

"And?" Ray asked.

"And I realized we've had a number of new volunteers this past year. What if one or more of them is associated with the killings? What if one of them is the so-called mastermind?"

"*Now you're thinking! There may be a murderer hiding amongst them,*" said Sherlock, as demanding as ever.

Bryan went over and hugged her. "Have I ever told you how brilliant you are?"

Ray smiled at the two of them and started looking through the folders. He had already set one aside as a possibility.

Two hours later, the volunteer applications were put in two piles. In the first pile there were a total of twelve people who had signed up to be volunteers within the last nine months, some who could possibly help Miranda. The second pile contained the names of those who had applied to be volunteers, but could be neither helpful to Miranda or were not qualified for volunteer activities at the zoo. Sometimes people had their hearts in the right place but were clueless about what would be expected of them. For example, it was really a nice thing to like animals!

"Check them all out for any history of criminal activity," Bryan told Ray.

"Now what?" asked Miranda

"Since I'm doing the research on the syndicate family, I'll give the names of those who filled out applications the past nine months to our computer genius and see if there are any connections. If that's okay with you two?" Both nodded their head yes.

"Good. I'm going home to my family. My wife is wondering if I have a girlfriend, I've been gone so much." Ray grinned and petted the dogs as he left.

"I'll need you to make copies of ones you're going to be checking and get originals back to me." Miranda shouted after him.

As Ray left, Bryan swung around, grabbed Miranda, held her tight, and kissed her. "You know love, it's getting more and more difficult for me to leave you."

"*You're going to have to give in sometime,*" said the three familiar voices in her head all at once.

Smiling, a glint in her eyes, she gently pushed him out the door and to his surprise told him, "Me too."

Chapter Thirty-Four

Volunteer Project

"*EMMA, THREE VOLUNTEERS WHO* are interested in working in the zoo hospital have agreed to meet me tomorrow afternoon. I'll bring the applications back later. I haven't gone through them all yet." The truth was, she was waiting for Officer Sanchez to bring them back after making copies. "I'll try to be there by noon."

Someone was banging at her door. The dogs were barking like crazy. The police officer from the car parked out front was holding on to a woman who was screaming, "Open the door and let me in."

"*Oh no, not her again,*" said Raymond.

It was Lillian Scott.

"Do you know this woman?" the officer asked.

"Unfortunately, I do, but she's not welcome here."

"Miranda, my home has been robbed. One of the horses on the ranch was murdered and a threatening note left for me to tell you and your father they want the money or else. Damn it, let me in."

Miranda gave the officer a nod. Lillian came inside, sat down, and began yelling, sounding more than a little paranoid, "Who is doing this to me. Is it Dennis? He won't take my calls. Jacob won't take my calls either."

"You're a filthy mess. What is wrong with you? I don't

know who is doing anything to you. And for your information, Dennis is dead. Someone murdered him."

Lillian finally shut up.

Miranda called Bryan to tell him her mother was here and what happened at her home outside of Taos.

"I'll be right there. Does she have the note they left her?" asked Bryan. He motioned to Ray to come with him, filling him in on the way about Lillian. "She's a piece of work."

Ray soon saw for himself. Lillian was sipping coffee, her hair looking like she had been electrocuted, and smelling like the dead horse on her ranch.

"I tried to get her to take a shower before you got here." Miranda, annoyed and rolling her eyes looked at the two men.

Bryan went over to Lillian. "Please do what Miranda is asking and I promise we'll help you stay safe." He was being soft and gentle. He realized she was totally traumatized. He had seen it many times before during his twelve years on the force.

"*He really is a good man,*" Agatha commented.

Lillian agreed to take a shower and put on the clean clothes Miranda gave her to wear. She came back downstairs acting less panicked but still very frightened. "Did Miranda show you the note they left? And what about my horse and the house?"

"We've contacted the Taos Sheriff and Police Departments. They're going to take care of everything including calling Animal Control," Ray told her after introducing himself.

Bryan handed Lillian a fresh cup of coffee and sat down next to her. "I have some questions. Are you alright to answer them?" He was wary of what she would say, having warned Ray earlier, "It's hard to know if what she says is true or not."

Miranda had interjected, "She's big on lying."

Lillian nodded yes to Bryan, and he began. "First of all, where have you been the past couple weeks?"

Ray made notes as Bryan questioned her.

"I stayed at the Mabel Dodge Lujan House. I never read a paper or listened to any news. I kept calling Dennis and Jacob."

"We know. Did anyone try to call you?"

"No."

"When did you go home?"

"Last night. When I saw what happened and read the note, I went back to the Lujan House, then I drove here as soon as it was light out today."

"Did you see anyone by the house when you got there? Or a car parked near it?" Bryan was being patient and letting Lillian take her time to answer.

"First, I saw the dead horse. Then I noticed the front door was broken open and inside the drawers and cupboards were trashed. The note was taped to the refrigerator. I didn't stay more than five minutes. I was so scared."

Miranda rolled her eyes. Even an amateur detective could tell some of what she was saying was a lie. Lillian's eyes were darting everywhere, and she kept wringing her hands.

"Why didn't you call for help last night?" Ray asked.

"Because even though I know my daughter's angry with me, I knew I could trust her to help me." She started to cry, but Miranda wasn't going to fall for her sob story.

"She's quite the actress," Raymond warned.

"Everyone is tired of your lies and cheating. I know for a fact you've annoyed the sheriff and police in Taos quite a few times. They probably would have ignored you. Remember, Mother, I lived with you on the ranch for many years." Miranda walked away from her to call Jacob. She wanted him to know Lillian had just shown up at her home and something about a threatening note left she had found inside her trashed home.

"Good for you, Miranda dear," said Agatha, lending her support.

Only Sherlock remained silent, waiting for more of the story to unfold.

It took another hour for Bryan and Ray to coax the truth from the increasingly defiant Lillian.

"Okay, okay! Yes! I heard Dennis had been murdered. It scared me so I left the ranch and stayed at a motel outside of Taos. Guess I did quite a bit of drinking and partying. I was running out of money, so I went home last night. Everything I told you I found when I got there is true."

Miranda was furious. "You need to find a place for her to stay. She can't stay here. I just spoke to Jacob, and he heard she had been drunk and acting crazy the past week. He also asked me what the note said, so I told him."

"Tell Leonard and Jacob we want the money they owe us, or you're dead like your horse. We'll be in touch. JP."

Lillian yelled and cursed, "I don't know where those two S.O.B.s are. They don't care what happens to me."

Miranda's father had told her years ago not to trust her mother, especially when it came to money or men. She sat down in front of Lillian and, in an accusing voice, asked her, "What aren't you telling us about you and Dennis that made you so scared when you heard he was murdered?"

Detective Anderson and Officer Sanchez didn't know Lillian Scott the way her daughter she did.

Even the worst of parents have a way of deceiving the outside world about their behavior, sometimes so cruel it's impossible to comprehend. Lillian was not among the worst, but she certainly was not among the best. She had men of all ages in and out of her bed when Leonard was away. She took money from them, and they sometimes hurt her when they discovered it.

There was, of course, much more she had done, which is also why Miranda was thrilled when she and her father moved to Albuquerque. It wasn't only because she wanted to go to school there and preferred being with her father. She wanted to be away from her mother.

"Yeah. This broad is definitely a nut job." Raymond reminded her.

"Clearly a compulsive liar," said Sherlock, more to the point.

All three of them stared at Lillian until she answered. "Dennis told me about his plans to blackmail the senator and said if I helped him, I could make a lot of money. When I heard he was murdered, I figured they might be looking to kill me too."

"Not a bad idea," Raymond remarked.

"Bryan, please get her out of here."

"Lillian, give me the keys to your car. Do you have any clothes with you?"

"Yes. In the car," handing Anderson the keys.

"I'm taking you to a safe house. A female police officer will be there to help you. Sanchez will take care of your car."

Answering his cell phone, saying yes several times, Bryan turned to Ray. "We need to get back to the station. Captain said Reed is asking for immunity if he agrees to tell what he knows about the senator's illegal activities."

As he was leaving, Ray turned to Lillian, disgusted by her. "Lady, you can pout, scream, whatever you want. You committed a crime planning to blackmail a senator."

***

As the door closed behind her mother, Miranda called Emma to tell her she wouldn't be in for the rest of the day. Then she made another call. "Can I come see you?"

Chapter Thirty-Five

Isabella

*L*ESS THAN TWENTY MILES northeast of Albuquerque, Placitas, once tribal grounds, was now a community of modestly priced homes and adobe mansions, laying claim to its landscape with beautiful views and miles of trails for hiking and biking. Centuries of heritage was built into this land where wild horses were known to roam.

It's their home too. Local residents agree.

Isabella Flores, half Anglo and half Hispanic, had been married to Jacob for over twenty-five years. Sometimes they lived together, other times not. They had their reasons, as we all do, in determining and accepting the kind of relationship we have with another person.

They brought an interesting family history together. Jacob Flores' mother was Jewish and his father was Hispanic. Their family gatherings were filled with a delicious variety of foods and a lot of humor, since half the people did not understand what the other half was saying. The food filled the void. So did love.

Embracing the differences, Isabella had created a series of children's books with lessons for children about tolerance and acceptance, about facing fears and being different. They were also about the importance of being kind to yourself, while still being kind to others.

Miranda loved the books and adored this woman who always gave her truth and understanding. She also loved being in her home. There was always a smell of fresh flowers in her house which was designed with pale walls surrounded by large windows, soft color furnishings, and artwork by New Mexico artists. The artwork offset the soft shades and gave the rooms charm and character with their bold colors. It was truly a home at home in its environment.

Sitting on a yellow sofa looking out at the mountains, Miranda asked, "Has Jacob told you what's been happening?"

"Yes." Isabella was sitting across from her on a beautiful flower-patterned yellow chair.

"Has my father been here too?

"Sometimes. Not often. He has to be careful." Isabella was worried Miranda would press her for information about him."

"Why?" Miranda had tears in her eyes.

"He'll be home soon."

"Do you think my father is a good man or a bad man?" It was a loaded question to ask about anyone, yet Miranda often wondered about her father.

"What do you think?" Isabella often answered a question by asking one.

"My father has always been good to me, but I believe sometimes good people do bad things," she answered.

"Miranda, do you think there is an issue of morality here and you're complicit somehow?"

"*I love this woman. So not like her crazy mother,*" said Raymond.

"Possibly. You're the philosophical thinker, Isabella. Is silence being complicit?"

"Not necessarily. Silence can be about protecting someone. It can also be fear of betraying someone. You never knew exactly what he was doing, so how could you be complicit?" Isabella understood her dilemma. "Leonard, Jacob, and a group of other men, including Fish, were involved in illegal activities revolving around high stakes bookmaking. That's not being a hardened criminal."

But what about now? Miranda got up to look out the window, a view of the mountains in the distance.

"In recent years, circumstances set them on a different path putting these men in harm's way. No, they are not hardened criminals—your words." Isabella also feared for Miranda. "I think we need some wine." Isabella got up. She didn't want Miranda to sense the concern she was feeling for her.

The wine mellowed them, taking the edge off the anxiety they had both begun feeling. It hadn't been an easy conversation. Miranda told Isabella, "I once asked a rabbi about the book, *Why Bad Things Happen to Good People* and wanted to know if he thought good things happen to bad people?"

"What did he tell you?"

"Isabella, he didn't tell me anything! He shrugged his shoulders and turned away. It made me angry and disappointed in him."

"I really don't have much of an answer either." Isabella told her. "There's been evil in the world since the beginning of time. The *Bible* blames it on Adam and Eve. Hard to know, except I believe there are people who are truly evil. Anyhow, speaking of evil, how is your not-so-charming mother?"

Miranda filled her in on what happened the past couple weeks and earlier in the day when Lillian came barging in telling lies to her and the police and begging for help.

"Where is the crazy lady now?" Isabella laughed.

"The police have taken her to a safe house. Really, she's crazier than ever and I refuse to be responsible for her."

"You don't need to be."

"What am I responsible for? Dead bodies found at the zoo? A sort of ex-boyfriend murdered, my mother ranting about being threatened, my father missing? Isabella, all *this* is what's really crazy. And why is it whatever my father is involved in has to be such a secret?"

"Maybe he's hiding out with some dame," said Raymond.

"Miranda, you're responsible for you. I bet your mystery writer friends have had a lot to say."

"Oh, them." Grinning, Miranda sat back on the yellow sofa. Her questions would not be answered, not yet. "They have often given me good advice, sometimes very wise advice."

Isabella grinned back and asked, "Do you have a favorite?"

"Hmmm. I love Raymond's toughness and Agatha's wisdom. When Sherlock is lecturing me, it's a bit annoying. But I do love his ability to get to the heart of the matter, to the truth of things. Like you."

Pouring them each more wine, the sun setting over the mountains, the whole landscape changing colors, Isabelle asked about Detective Anderson. "That's becoming very tricky," said Miranda with that glint in her eye again!

Chapter Thirty-Six

Father and Daughter Memories

IT WAS NEARLY MIDNIGHT when Miranda arrived home. She had ignored calls from Bryan and Emma and one only a half hour ago from George Perez. Concerned why he was calling so late, she checked his message before going into the house. "Emma asked me to try to find you. The lady lion is in labor and its way before her time."

She knew her neighbor would have taken care of the dogs, so she turned around back to the car, waved to the policeman parked out front of her house and texted a message to Bryan, Emma, and George. "I'm on my way to the zoo."

Bryan arrived minutes after she did, yelling, "With everything bad happening, don't disappear like that again. I've been worried to death."

"Oh how sweet," Raymond commented rather sarcastically.

"You're the one making this relationship tricky darling," Agatha sounding pushy.

"Well, it certainly is a bit difficult having a romantic relationship with a detective when your father and friends have a history of being gangsters!" added Sherlock uncharacteristically.

"Oh, shut up, all of you!" Miranda muttered under her

breath, causing Bryan to smile.

Once again Bryan and Miranda would be waiting for a baby or, in this case, babies to be born. George, two of the lionkeepers, and the vet tech were already at the lion habitat.

"I'll give her a couple more hours at the most. After that, I'll do a C-section. George, thanks for getting everyone here. You and the vet tech go to the hospital and check that everything is ready for surgery, in case it becomes necessary. Emma texted me she'll be in her office if we need her."

Miranda checked her watch, keeping track of Kamali's labor. The lionkeepers had separated her from Kasi who was pacing like many expectant fathers.

"Where were you?" Bryan wanted to know, still annoyed with Miranda.

"He's worried about you. Be nice to him," Agatha reminded her.

"I'm sorry. Really, I am. After my mother's insane visit, I needed to talk to a friend. I went to see Jacob's wife, Isabella. I'm sure you know they have a home in Placitas," Miranda said a bit playfully.

"I do." Putting his arm around her, "I'm sorry too. I know these past few weeks have been difficult for you. Did you tell her how crazy you are about me?"

Hesitating for a moment, Miranda kissed him on the lips. "I told her what a pain in the rear you are."

"Hey, I'm adorable," he protested. Miranda was doing her best to control her emotions. She thought he was adorable too, but this was hardly the time for a romantic moment.

Bryan forced himself to change the subject, at least for the time being. "I assume you talked about your father?"

"We did and she said she couldn't tell me anything.

I have so many memories of my father and being his daughter. Driving home, I remembered when I was about nineteen. I was out dancing with some friends. A guy I knew was getting overly aggressive and obnoxious with me and I finally said to him, 'You do know who my father is?'"

"And?" Bryan wanted to know what happened.

"He walked right away." Miranda grinned.

"Sometimes I'd wake up and find my father left a gift next to my bed. It was always something he heard me say I liked. One time, there was the complete volumes of Shakespeare and another time there were a couple of beautiful cashmere sweaters."

"Spoiled brat?" Bryan commented with a huge smile.

"Spoiled, yes. Brat, no. He made sure I would not become a brat. He taught me about generosity and to understand the world is different for a woman than a man. He was also big on being respected. But..." Miranda didn't finish what she was saying. She was startled by the loud and piercing roar of the male lion.

She texted George, "We need to bring Kamali to the hospital immediately! Something is wrong."

It took everyone available to bring the lady lion to the hospital after Miranda gave her a sedative. No one wants to get into a cage with a lion who is awake, plus in labor. Forty minutes later, Miranda finished the C-section. She gave her a shot for pain and another with antibiotics as a preventative measure, before she was taken to a place where she could recover from the surgery.

Miranda texted Emma, "Kamali had two premature female cubs. Kasi will have to wait for mother and cubs to join him. I hear him roaring like a proud father."

The detective and veterinarian would also have to wait for romantic time together. The mysteries facing them were a serious threat.

Two days after the birth of the lion cubs, Isabella called. "Miranda, if it's okay with you, I'd like to spend some time with you."

Easy to know whose idea it was. Jacob and Leonard.

Her large overnight bag said it was more than just some time. Miranda was thrilled. Bryan was relieved.

The person overseeing the syndicate's revenge was troubled. It complicated their plans.

Chapter Thirty-Seven

Revenge

*T*HE *PROBLEM WITH REVENGE* is it distorts a person's rational thinking, and while it is intended to inflict harm on someone else, it invariably finds its way back home.

The local press wrote a scathing story. "Senator Matthew Graham is accused of raising money for his political campaigns and diverting large sums to his personal accounts. In addition, he is accused of arranging for Detective Thomas Wilson to kill Dennis Huxley. Huxley was attempting to blackmail him. Both Detective Wilson and Carl Reed, the senator's associate, received large sums of money from him."

"The press doesn't have all the information, not yet. Reed is willing to tell all but he's requesting immunity. Graham will want his head. We need to put the pieces of this puzzle together before someone else is murdered." Bryan was tired and frustrated by the endless circle of deception and violence.

Ray was equally frustrated. "Graham is out on bail. He's unapologetic, constantly swearing he's not guilty, and saying it was all Reed's idea. The lawyers and courts will have to settle this mess."

"This mess includes my dear mother," said Miranda,

understandably furious. "Presently she is in a safe house, but I assume at some point she'll be charged with helping Huxley plan to blackmail the senator."

"She should be behind bars," remarked Sherlock.

"I doubt she'll do any jail time, maybe some community service. It depends if the judge is sympathetic or not," Bryan remarked. No one felt any sympathy for the lady, especially Sherlock.

At Miranda's, Bryan spread out the photos of the Powell brothers on the table below the index cards. "They're a charming pair. They murdered the two people at the zoo and Karla. The attempted kidnapper, Zach Powell (a first cousin) is in jail."

"Their indifference to human life is staggering." Isabella, Miranda's houseguest, found it difficult to comprehend such irrational and vindictive behavior. She asked the others, "Any idea who is directing all this?"

"Not entirely," Bryan replied. "The head of the defunct east coast business syndicate probably sent the Powell's here to demand and extort the money they say Leonard and Jacob owe them. They've failed miserably. I believe there are people in New Mexico involved and they'll probably go to extremes to get what they want. We need to figure out who they are."

"You mean the murders and attempted kidnapping haven't been extreme enough?" asked Isabella.

"They're desperate. No telling what they're liable to do next." Bryan had taken Miranda's hand.

"The list of syndicate families and their siblings should be completed soon. The research became complicated since many of the children changed their last names, some even moved out of the country. Also, I made copies of all the volunteers in the folder Miranda gave me and I'll cross-reference them with the other lists," Ray told them.

"Too few people are what they seem," Agatha said firmly.

"I reviewed information on the zoo volunteers who began the past eight or nine months. Isabella said she would help and go through them tomorrow to see if anything seems off to her in their applications. If any volunteers' names match any on Ray's lists, it would certainly raise a huge red flag of worry." Miranda handed Isabella her volunteer folder.

"It seems to me it would be beneficial to create stories to build mistrust and doubt in their mind," said Isabella. The other three smiled at her.

Isabella added, "Maybe comments like, we have several good leads on finding the Powell Brothers."

"Or it looks like Zach Powell is about to talk," added Raymond.

"Great idea!" Miranda yawned.

It was late and, truly, enough was enough for now.

Before leaving, Bryan put his arm around Miranda. "How about some alone time?"

Poor guy didn't know what was going on with their relationship. An occasional kiss and hug seemed pretty darn skimpy!

Isabella overheard and laughed. "Take Bryan with you to lunch at the ranch."

"Take her advice," stated Agatha.

"The guy's going to be furious you didn't tell him," added Raymond.

"And he has every right to be, thank you!" said Sherlock.

"What lunch?" Bryan was immediately anxious... and annoyed.

"The rancher whose horse I operated on invited me to lunch, said he wants to talk to me about an idea for the

Rescue Center."

"Where's his ranch?" Bryan's voice had actually gone up several octaves.

"It's not far past the Rescue and Retirement Center, and you can stop there first." Isabella answered. She was truly enjoying this moment.

"Not without me. Not after all that's been happening." Bryan was not happy!

"Great, we can both take a sick day. Pick me up at 9 a.m. the day after tomorrow." Smiling, Miranda put her arm around Isabella and whispered, "Thank you."

Pleased with herself Isabella suggested, "Ray, while they go off to the ranch, maybe we could make a hit list of who to intimidate a bit."

Ray agreed. He couldn't wait to tell his wife about this interesting woman. Then again, he thought it might not be such a good idea!

Chapter Thirty-Eight

The Ranch Visit

DRIVING NORTH FROM ALBUQUERQUE, the swirling clouds promised rain desperately needed by the farmers and ranchers. The drought was taking a heavy toll on the land and the animals, affecting lives and their livelihood.

Garrett Bishop and his wife, whom he lovingly called Ruthie, welcomed Miranda and Bryan to their 40-acre ranch as if they were old friends. Their warmth was everywhere. The ranch house was painted a shade of light tan, the doors and window trimmings a deeper shade. The entire home was surrounded by a garden someone obviously spent hours caring for. Different flowering plants and fruit trees framed the house with the front window facing the fields where the Bishops could see their beloved horses.

Inside the immaculate home, the two guests went into a dining room where flowered wallpaper walls were covered with dozens of photos of their horses. Some were of children riding them, some were of mares with their foals, and many were photos Garrett Bishop had taken of Ruthie riding Chrystal, a beautiful chestnut colored mare.

"This is what love looks like," Agatha commented.

"We never could have children, so we love our horses like family."

Miranda was enthralled by the photos, telling Garrett, "You should put some of these photos on display at the Rescue Center. They really are beautiful."

Ten minutes later Ruthie shouted from the kitchen. "I hope you like Mexican food!"

The delicious meal was shared in a home filled with love and memories. Miranda only had this kind of home life after she and her father left her mother behind and moved to Albuquerque. She realized Bryan never talked about what it was like for him growing up, only that he had been adopted. He made it clear it was not a topic he was willing to discuss. At least not yet.

Bryan was so moved by this couple he smiled and reached over and took Miranda's hand, as Garrett Bishop explained their idea. "Ruthie and I are both getting older. Our ranch has done quite well financially, and I would like to set up a fund for the rescue center. Miranda, I was so impressed by the care and concern you had for my horse."

"Don't forget how impressed you were by how she treated you," Ruthie commented. Bryan squeezed Miranda's hand, so proud of her.

"True. Very true." Garrett got up and brought over an album filled with photos of beautiful horses they had owned over the years.

"Many have passed on, many others we've recently given to another rancher in the area who we know will take good care of them. Plus, we can visit them." Ruthie had tears in her eyes.

"We have kept a couple of our favorites," Garrett told them, going on to explain, "There would be one specific requirement for the center. They would need to hire a full-time veterinarian."

"You know I couldn't possibly..." Miranda started to say.

"Sounds like a wise decision. Women!" said Raymond, voicing his negative thoughts as usual.

"Oh be quiet for a change. This is a time to listen," said Agatha, forcefully for her.

Ruthie stopped her. "Oh no darling, we're not asking you. We're hoping you would help us set up this program and oversee how the donation is spent."

"We hope you would be a consultant for the program, making sure the funding is used for what it's being designated. Of course, we wouldn't expect you to do this for free. Part of the funding would include a consulting fee." Garrett sighed, looked at Ruthie and smiled.

"Before you say anything else, it's clearly time for dessert." Ruthie placed cups of coffee and slices of homemade chocolate cake on the table.

"This cake is incredible. You've convinced me to do anything you want," grinned Bryan.

"He's right. It is amazing. So is your idea. I'll talk to the Center's Executive Director, and she'll take it to the board. I can't imagine they'll refuse because they need a full-time veterinarian. I'm only able to visit a couple times a month and for emergencies. Garrett, I have a couple questions?" Miranda was genuinely enthused.

Garrett jumped in saying, "How much money will we donate and how will the funding work? One of the reasons we need your involvement is to help make those decisions. Next question?"

Miranda stood up and went to look at the photos on the wall as Bryan looked through the photo album on the table. "They have a lovely visitor's center, where people can pick up information and buy a variety of animal related gifts. The money from sales goes to care of the animals. Would you be willing to hang some of your photos there and allow us to make prints of them to sell?"

Ruthie could hardly contain herself. She got up and went over to give Miranda a hug and quietly told her, "I think your boyfriend is a hunk!"

Bryan wanted to know, "Why are you two laughing so hard?"

Garrett heard the comment, but decided to mind his own business, except to say, "Seems as if this idea could work out very nicely."

It was late afternoon when they headed back to Albuquerque. The rain had begun, lightly at first. Then they heard thunder and knew it would get heavier as the winds picked up.

"I want to stop at the Rescue Center to tell them about the Bishops' offer."

Bryan checked in with Ray, while Miranda explained the offer and discussed a few options and how she would be involved.

Over an hour later, they were heading back to the city. The roads were wet and slippery, and the earlier clouds had darkened, promising more rain. The clouds appeared ominous. Still, they were beautiful, constantly adding shades of purple and grey to the sky.

It was always easy for Miranda's mind to wander, especially during weather like this.

The problem with heavy rainstorms in New Mexico is the flooding which can cause water rushing into the arroyos. For some reason, foolishly some people get caught up in them and are swept away in the rushing water.

Thank goodness her world had nothing to do with floods. There were other worries to consider, but not right now. Sitting close to Bryan, Miranda leaned over to kiss him on the cheek. "It feels different heading into the city than leaving it. The mountain seems to be hovering to protect it and looking west there are changing shadows spreading across the landscape."

Bryan pulled her closer, asking, "You like the Bishops, don't you?"

"I do," Miranda replied.

"Careful with those two words. Could get you in trouble." Bryan had a huge smile.

Quickly changing the subject, Miranda asked if he liked the Bishops' idea for the rescue center?

"I do."

"Now *you're* in trouble."

Chapter Thirty-Nine

Volunteers Meeting

*E*ARLY THE NEXT MORNING, Miranda walked the zoo grounds to check on the animals, concerned about several who would need medical treatment next week. Her meeting with the vet techs and several volunteers interested in working with them had been rescheduled for this morning.

Before leaving for work she asked Isabella, "Do you and Ray think any of the volunteers are a threat? I saw the applications spread across the kitchen counter when I got home last night."

"Possibly. Ray is checking further on a couple of them. We decided we should all meet here tonight. Meantime, you look...well, you look happy."

Miranda grinned confirming it was true.

Isabella gave her a hug goodbye. "Wish me luck, I have a meeting at the main library about my children's books."

Miranda hugged her back. "Wonderful. I hope you have to spend a lot more time here."

The meeting with the volunteers was not wonderful. She had to tell one of the women, "I appreciate your wanting to work with the care of the animals, but I think this might not be the best fit for you... or us. We could use your help some other way."

The woman went ballistic, cursing Miranda and telling her aliens were going to get her. George Perez was called to escort her off the grounds and take away her volunteer badge. She was not happy.

Emma, hearing the screaming, texted Miranda, "Need help?"

Miranda replied, "No. But let's go for lunch. I'll meet you back here at 12:30."

They had lunch at the Range Café on Rio Grande Boulevard. The restaurant was close to the zoo, the food was good, and the staff didn't throw them out if they sat there talking for a long time.

They discussed the idea for the rescue center, the volunteers, the lion cubs and possible names, and when Kamali and the cubs could be together again with Kasi.

"Since it was a caesarian birth, let's give her another week. Have Deidre invite the press. There could be some great photos of their reunion." Miranda grinned.

"Ok, come on, you're not grinning only because of the lions getting together," Emma teased her.

"Sort of true. I guess it's Bryan's influence. We had a good time together yesterday." Miranda was still smiling.

"He went with you?" Emma asked, surprised.

"He's concerned my life is still in danger."

"Makes sense. Have you heard any more about who committed the murders at the zoo? I saw the photos on the news of two guys considered suspects."

"Not yet." Miranda remembered Isabella's suggestion. "They have a lead on where they are and who's been pulling their strings."

"Sounds good, Miranda."

A short time later, Emma stood up and took the check. "I need to get back to the zoo for a meeting."

The rain started again in the late afternoon and continued off and on for several hours. By the time Ray and Bryan got to her house, thank goodness with pizza and wine, the rain had slowed to a drizzle. Miranda let the dogs out and opened the doors so they could enjoy the cool evening breeze.

Ray took a couple slices of pizza out to a very appreciative officer in the police car who was watching the house. When he came back, Bryan was looking through the volunteer files and asked him, "When can we have the lists of the syndicate kids' names. Not much we can do with these until we have them."

"Unless one tries to attack me at the hospital," Miranda joked.

Bryan didn't find it the least bit funny.

Chapter Forty

I'm Not Guilty

THE NEXT DAY TURNED out to not be very funny either. Carl Reed was found dead in his cell. The captain was infuriated. "It most certainly wasn't suicide! Seems the senator has a long reach. Bryan, get him in here."

Once again, the arrogant senator proclaiming his innocence appeared with his attorney.

"Guess he felt guilty, so he killed himself. Like I told you, he was the bad guy, not me."

"We have a search warrant for your phone and computer. Reed was murdered." Bryan tossed the warrant in front of him and his attorney.

"What the hell! I had nothing to do with it. I was home all night. Ask my protection detail." Oh, how he did protest!

"You tell your client I want his phone right now and an officer will go home with him to get the computer. If he refuses, he'll be arrested again." Bryan put his hand across the table waiting for the senator's phone.

Being incredibly belligerent, the senator practically threw it at him. "Let's get out of here." The senator stood up, pushed his chair to the floor, and walked out leaving an embarrassed attorney to follow after him.

Ray had watched the interview. "I'm going with the officer to get the computer. I know we need to see if he contacted anyone to arrange a hit on Reed."

More and more the detective was impressed by Sanchez. "Thanks, I'll check his phone."

***

If all this wasn't enough fun, another person was screaming not guilty and demanding to go home. "She's a damn pain and if she wants to go home, I say let her," said the female officer who had called the detective after being on guard with her all morning and listening to her abusive tirades.

"I'll be right over." Bryan didn't object to Lillian Scott going home. It was Miranda who was in danger.

"Your mother is demanding to go home. Are you okay with it?"

"*Send the crazy dame home,*" Raymond shouted.

"If it's okay with you, I'm fine with it as long as she stays away from me."

Bryan called the office and asked to speak to her. "Lillian, you'll have to come back here in a month or two to face charges of attempted bribery. Don't even say no or complain. If you fail to show up, there will be an arrest warrant for you. Understood?"

Detective Anderson didn't want to hear any more of her nonsense. He arranged for her car kept in police custody to be delivered to a location away from the safe house and told the officer to give her the keys. With that, Lillian Scott disappeared again. Not that anyone cared.

Back at the station Ray was waiting for him with Senator Graham's computer. Together they went through his emails and calls on his cell phone. A few seemed suspicious but, after following up on them, nothing seemed to link the senator to the murder of Reed.

"I'm sure he's involved. Find out what officers were on duty last night and if Reed had any visitors the past couple days." Bryan was heading to talk to the captain to update him on the senator and Lillian. Thanks to the female police officer, Miranda's mother was now officially being called Lady Macbeth. Shakespeare would have been appalled.

Chapter Forty-One

More Craziness

"**W**AKE UP! *SOMEONE'S AT* the door and the dogs are going crazy!" shouted Isabella. Miranda squinted to look at the clock. It was 5:30 in the morning. The sun was barely beginning to greet the day and the police officer on overnight duty watching her house was holding on tight to the volunteer who had caused such a fuss at the zoo the day before.

Isabella went downstairs to make coffee while waiting for another police car to come by with two officers to collect the woman. "She told the police she followed you home after you left work and was demanding to see you."

The police left a message for Detective Anderson following his instructions to let him know of any problems at Miranda's house. "Maybe I'll go back to bed. Wake me when it's Christmas!" said Miranda. The two women laughed, enjoyed talking and drinking coffee, as the early morning sunrise colored the sky.

"I'm going with you to the zoo until we know who this woman is. First, a quick stop at the library to drop off some of my books. They're interested in my offering programs on writing for children."

"How often?"

"Depends on if the program is only at the main library

or if they also want it at several of the branches." Isabella had her own plans.

"Fine, but first my treat at the Range Café for breakfast." Miranda was sure Jacob and her father were behind the idea of Isabella staying in the city. She loved the idea.

"Smart family!" said Sherlock.

"Isabella is certainly up to something more than books." Raymond commented sarcastically.

Meantime, Bryan had left Miranda a message. "We're doing a background check on the volunteer trying to see you this morning. We're especially interested if she has a criminal record or is related in some way to the syndicate back east. I'll try to stop by the zoo later. Please be careful." Concern was evident in his voice.

It was also understandable considering the replies the police had after showing the photos of the two men on the news.

The zoo was quiet and the day warming up when Miranda and Isabella got there a little after 10 a.m., and true to the Albuquerque popular weather motto, "If you don't like the weather, wait ten minutes."

Emma, her office door opened, waved to them then turned away. The vet tech handed Miranda a list of which animals were having medical exams the following week and the volunteers assigned to assist. George Perez stopped to say, "The lion cubs are being very playful. They're so darn cute. Do we have names for them yet?"

George usually made his first rounds of the Zoo grounds before 9 in the morning, so he could let Miranda know if any animal might need immediate attention that day.

"Soon, hopefully. We discussed when we'll move Kamali and the cubs with Kasi. Also, George, please check on the zebra's habitat and be sure the new fence is high enough to keep out unwanted visitors. There's always some idiot who wants to get in to pet the newborn." Miranda thanked him and texted Bryan to see if he had any information on the crazy volunteer.

Isabella put her arm around her. "Darling, you're going to make a great mother someday."

Miranda glared at her and then joked, "You first." She was not prepared for *that* conversation. Not with anyone!

Miranda felt like it was an endlessly long day waiting to hear back from Bryan. Checking on different animals, Isabella walking with her mentioned, "Emma seemed remote this morning and Perez certainly overly accommodating. Maybe I'm the crazy one. I think I'm getting suspicious of everyone around here. Except you, of course."

"*Everyone should be considered suspicious,*" said Raymond putting in his two cents.

It was late afternoon when Bryan called. "Sorry, I didn't get to the zoo. We've been dealing with Reed's murder. Sanchez took care of the crazy volunteer problem, and she is just that. Crazy. She has a long history of mental problems, stalking and attacking people, damaging their property, at least no murders. Not to worry about her, she's been placed in care of her family, and they've been told if she attempts to see you again, she'll be arrested."

"Wonderful, thanks! I'll tell Isabella. Crazy lady had us up bright and early, so no meeting tonight if that's okay with you. Anyhow, we're all waiting for Ray to have the complete list of children's names related to the syndicate family."

"Aww, you think I'm wonderful." Bryan was laughing.

"Aww, I'm going to hang up. Oh, wait! What's happening with Reed's murder?"

Isabella was listening, wondering when the two of

them would realize how much they cared for each other.

"The police officer on duty has been placed on paid leave although we don't think he was involved, but it's protocol. We're sure someone visiting the jail managed to kill him. Eventually, we'll get them. A couple of officers are looking through videos of visitors now," Bryan told her.

"Do you think the senator put someone up to it?" Miranda asked as she and Isabella walked over to see the lion cubs who were sleeping peacefully against their mother.

"Yes. Ray and I are convinced he was. Meantime, hopefully we'll be ready to meet tomorrow evening. Oh yeah. Lock your doors and don't let anyone in unless it's wonderful me." Bryan was really getting to Miranda, and he loved it.

Fortunately, no one came knocking at Miranda's door after they came home. Being two very intelligent women, they stopped to pick up dinner along with treats for her dogs. The evening was spent watching an old black and white movie they loved and had both seen many times, *Laura*. The dogs were snug together between them, paper cartons of food put away, and each comfortable and calm for a change.

At two in the morning, Miranda wasn't sure if it was a bad dream waking her or a voice shouting in her head.

"It's your business to know what other people don't!" shouted Sherlock again.

It was forgotten for now as she fell back to sleep.

Chapter Forty-Two

The Powells

THE INVESTIGATION OF THE zoo murders was about to change. The Powell brothers were getting desperate. They'd been hiding in the mountains. Their money was gone and they'd run out of food. More troubling, no one had contacted them about getting out of New Mexico safely. They realized they were no longer under the protection of the old man back east and, instead, were now being hunted not just by the Albuquerque police, but by the unknown New Mexico contact, as well.

Jaxson Powell was insufferable. Feeling forced to give himself up, and now being interrogated, he became increasingly vulgar and combative. His brother, Peter, in a different room, was mostly scared and disoriented. Neither man had showered or eaten a decent meal in over a week.

Detective Anderson asked one of the officers to bring them some sandwiches, cookies, and sodas hoping it would help them calm down. They could get cleaned up later. First, Detectives Anderson and Sanchez wanted to find out if the two brothers gave the same story.

The stupidity and ineptness of their behavior proved to be almost beyond comprehension. Sanchez played the recordings of their stories to the captain, and it was agreed they were too similar to be telling lies. Jaxson's language, however, was certainly more colorful than his brother's.

"Months ago, we were invited to meet with the man who headed the business syndicate years ago. He heard people were restarting the bookkeeping scheme, same as the type Leonard Scott and Jacob Flores had made millions doing years before. He was convinced Scott and Flores were involved and it infuriated the old man. Told us he already placed a couple people in Albuquerque. It was his damn, stupid idea to send Karla and my cousin Zach ahead of us."

"Did you help Karla before she came here?" Sanchez asked.

"Yeah. I had a guy redo her resume and make her a new ID. We needed Karla to get a job at the zoo and meet any single men that worked there. After the kidnapping fiasco, Karla was afraid of getting caught and panicked. You understand, I had to kill her. The dumb broad was getting ready to leave. The old man probably would have killed me if I didn't."

Ray clicked off the recording. "Both admitted to killing the guy found in the lions' habitat and John Lynch. They said someone in Albuquerque told them what to do. So far, they've refused to say who."

Clicking the recorder back on, "We figured dumping Karla's body by Miranda Scott's house would give her father a good scare. Then we left threatening notes for her and even drove all the way to Taos one day to scare her mother. While we were there, we trashed the house. It was a *friggin* mess anyhow. Before we left, we shot the horse for the hell of it."

Stopping the recorder again, Ray told them, "They really are disgusting. Wait till you hear the rest."

"I want to know what scared these morons into hiding?" The captain was shaking his head in disbelief.

"Here's the rest of it." Ray set the recorder on the captain's desk.

"Peter and I decided to hell with the old man. We were going after the money ourselves. Then we got a call from the old man, telling us not to worry, he'd find a way to take care of us. We didn't believe him."

"Why not? Sanchez had asked him.

"Mostly because he's an S.O.B. and suddenly was so nice to us. B.S. And we were right not to believe him. Someone shot at us when we were leaving a fast-food restaurant. Peter was hurt, but not too bad. I dragged him into the car, and we drove as fast as we could out of the city. All our clothes and personal things are still at our apartment. We stayed in the car the first night. The next few days we stayed in a cheap motel until we ran out of money. Now, here we are in a damn mess."

"You certainly are that and more," Detective Anderson had responded.

"Yeah, but we got some bargaining power."

"Doubtful."

"Wouldn't you like to know who's really in charge in Albuquerque? Peter needs some medical care. We want protection and an attorney."

***

The two were taken to the same safe house Lillian Scott had just left. A doctor saw to Peter's wound. Their apartment was searched by forensics and clothes from the apartment were brought to them, and a legal aid attorney was assigned to their case.

News of their arrest was sure to push whoever was running the operation in Albuquerque into swift and dangerous actions.

Chapter Forty-Three

The Lists

ONE OF THE ZOO volunteers was on the list of people related to the syndicate.

"The Queens Business Syndicate was the name filed in court proceedings. At one time they had close to a hundred members. True, less than a dozen of them, all men, were in the top tier of the organization." Ray handed Bryan and the captain the list.

"You can see one man was the head of it. The names of everyone's children are listed, including their married names."

"What about the zoo volunteer list?"

Ray handed a copy to both men. One of the volunteers was on the list of people related to the syndicate. All three men were shocked at another name on the list.

Anderson immediately called, then texted Miranda. "Go home and stay there. Will explain later." There was no answer to either.

Bryan Anderson was a good detective with great instincts when it came to police matters. "Ray, we need to get to the zoo."

George Perez was the first to see the two men rushing into the zoo followed by several police cars pulling into the parking lot. "Where are Miranda and Emma?" Anderson shouted.

"Haven't seen them for the past couple hours," said Perez looking puzzled by all the police activity.

Ray rushed over to him, "We'll explain later. Close down the zoo. No visitors for the rest of the day. Get your security guards to help us look for Emma and Miranda. Check Emma's office first, then the Visitor's Center and cafe. Afterwards, search the grounds."

At the same time, Anderson made a call to Isabella, "Miranda is missing, I'm sure she's in trouble. We know who's been in charge of the murders and the Powells. Call Jacob, tell him and Fish we could use their help at the zoo." A couple of old-time gangsters could be helpful.

The zoo hospital had three treatment rooms, another with an x-ray machine and other testing equipment, and a surgery area. Ray pushed the door open to the surgery area and turned to find Bryan, "You'd better see this." Sanchez was staring at a very pretty woman... a very pretty dead woman. Her volunteer badge revealed one of the names they had found on the list of people related to the syndicate.

Bryan was doing his best to stay calm, thinking of Miranda as he looked at this woman, obviously murdered. "Call forensics. Tell them we need a coroner and an ambulance, Ray. Just in case."

Ray completely understood. More and more he was proving himself as someone the detective could rely on, especially in an emergency. And probably as a friend. Bryan told two more police officers who came into the hospital, "Wait for the coroner and forensics and help officer Sanchez secure the crime scene. The dead woman was murdered with a knife from a sterile surgery operating packet that was ripped open. There should be plenty of fingerprints on the knife. Be sure they get photos."

Perez rushed in, saw the body, and turned to Detective Anderson. "We didn't find the women, but we haven't checked the hidden habitat entrances. We'll need your help, there's so many of them."

"What?" The detective didn't know what George was talking about.

"Zookeepers have a hidden entrance they use to clean the animal areas, feed them, and even work out ways to connect with them," Perez quickly explained.

All hell had broken loose at the zoo. The coroner, more police cars, and the ambulance arrived. Jacob, Fish, and Isabella rushed in ahead of them, Jacob shouting, "Any idea where she is?" Outside the media had formed a crowd shouting questions.

Shaking his head Perez said, "There are hidden entrances for all the habitats. Who the hell knows where to start?"

"Good grief," Isabella said, "The lions' habitat. Miranda recently took me through the hidden entrance and down some steps to show me what goes on behind the scenes."

"Police are at the zoo's hospital because there's a dead woman in the surgery area."

Fish looked at the detective dumbfounded and asked, "Is it Emma or Miranda?"

"Neither. We're not sure where they are. Take us to the lion habitat's entrance." They all started running, fearful of what might be happening.

Seeing Miranda's staff card lying on the top step scared them to death!

"She's down here!" Bryan was doing his best to not let his personal feelings get in the way of what he needed to do, but he truly felt like he was going into the lion's den.

Jacob and Fish followed. They weren't sure who they could trust, but they weren't taking any chances.

Isabella, fearing the worst, made a decision and a phone call.

"Leonard, Miranda's in trouble."

Chapter Forty-Four

Emma and Miranda

TWO HOURS EARLIER, EMMA called Miranda. "I need your input on the plans for the new visitor viewing section. Also, let's check on Kamali and her cubs to be sure they can be moved soon. Can you meet me for coffee?"

"Sure. I'll meet you at the café in half an hour." Miranda knew the expansion was an exciting addition for the zoo. It was being developed to increase attendance and, more importantly, to make it easier and safer for visitors to view many of the larger animals.

The Albuquerque afternoons were getting warmer as days got longer. Many of the animals were asleep in areas shaded and cool. In a few months, the summer heat would have its way with people and animals. Shade would be needed for everyone. Two volunteers walked by them with a group of giggling children touring the Zoo.

Miranda and Emma had left the café, stopped to say hello to them and asked if they saw the new baby zebra. There were questions and more giggling as the children moved on. The innocence of childhood... one could only hope it would stay that way for a long time.

Nothing was ever as perfect as it seemed, or one hoped it was. Miranda's mind was racing, she knew something wasn't right. So did the voices in her head. Emma's behavior in the café seemed irrational and so unlike the Emma she had known for the past ten years.

Sherlock's words once again were, *"There is nothing more deceptive than an obvious fact. Be sure to see what is obvious here."*

"Listen to Sherlock," both Raymond and Agatha seemed to be telling her, as well.

They headed to the lions' habitat. The areas below were, of course, familiar to both the curator and senior veterinarian, but were intentionally meant to be unseen by visitors. It was part of their jobs to provide excellent care and healthy homes for the animals at this zoo, without interference from strangers. The two women had done a good job together and the zoo had prospered in every way.

Raymond began to shout quite loudly in Miranda's head, *"Damn it! Remember what Sherlock said, watch for the obvious."*

What was obvious to Miranda was the need to be very cautious. As they walked down the steps taking them to the inner workings of the lions' habitat, Miranda slipped off her identification tag and tossed it behind her onto the first step. She always wore it when she was at the zoo.

Everyone who worked there knew it.

Kamali's cubs stayed close to her as they saw the two women. She roared loudly to express her uncertainty at their being there. The roars would soon bring Kasi nearby wanting to protect them.

Emma was staring at the lions as if she, too, was uncertain what to do next when Miranda asked her,

"Why did you lie to me?"

"When?" Emma had her hand in her pocket.

"When you told me after lunch at the Range that you

had a meeting to get to. Earlier in the day, you said you would be staying late only to finish a couple grants you were working on," Miranda reminded her.

"Maybe I changed my mind." Emma paused to look around.

"No one else is here Emma. Only you and me. What's wrong?"

"I have a feeling you know." Emma almost seemed sad for the moment.

"I'm not sure, but I think I do." Miranda moved to whisper to Kamali to calm her.

"I'm responsible for the murders of four people... and now." Emma stopped talking.

"And now you feel you have to murder me? Why?"

"You wouldn't understand. I was forced to do it. He's an awful man." Emma pulled a gun out of her pocket.

"Told you!" Raymond shouted.

"Keep her talking and stay calm. You know someone will see your name tag on the step." Sherlock was so rational.

"Be careful, Talk softly and slowly. Don't upset her." Agatha sounded worried.

"Who's an awful man? The police will help you if someone has been hurting you or threatening you."

Miranda was doing her best to keep Emma engaged until someone found them. She knew Isabella or Bryan would be trying to reach her. They would realize what was obvious, something was very wrong.

"Did you kill the men who we found murdered here at the zoo?" asked Miranda.

"Just a little longer. Bryan will find you," said Agatha, trying to be encouraging.

"Watch her every move! This dame has been running the show the whole time!" Raymond was urging Miranda

to be alert.

"They were murdered on my order. Well, really his order. Except for the volunteer in the surgery area today. I had to kill her myself. The Powell brothers, they're both so damn stupid! I arranged to have you kidnaped and ransomed. Would you believe those idiots he sent to help me?" Emma sounded bitter and was getting more and more agitated.

"Emma," Miranda asked calmly trying to express concern rather than fear. "Who ordered you to do these terrible things?"

Suddenly, Kamali let out several terrifying roars, frightening her cubs. She had heard the noises at the entrance, then loud footsteps rushing down to where Emma and Miranda were. The men moved cautiously. Several of them had never been so near a lion, especially one that was not very happy at the moment.

Seeing Emma holding a gun pointed at Miranda, Detective Anderson spoke quietly. "Emma, you know me, let me help you. The zoo has been closed and there are police with the forensics team and the coroner at the zoo hospital. We're all scaring the lions." He knew how fragile negotiations like this could be.

Emma suddenly grabbed Miranda, screaming and pointing at Jacob. "What are you doing here? It's your fault. If you would have given him the money he wanted, none of this would have happened. I should shoot you. I should shoot all of you."

Jacob wasn't afraid of her. People more dangerous than her had pointed guns at him.

"Emma, he's been lying to you. We gave him a great deal of money years ago. He's an angry old man who's going to die broke and unimportant by his own actions."

Emma didn't move as Jacob softly told her, "I think

you know I'm telling you the truth. He's a bad man who gets pleasure out of hurting people, even you."

Everyone stood very still, not sure what Emma would do next. Suddenly, she pushed Miranda down, quickly turned, and ran through the back of the habitat and out a second hidden entrance. Bryan and Jacob followed her, very carefully. The woman did have a gun!

Perez and Fish took Miranda upstairs to a grateful Isabella. As they walked toward the zoo entrance, they saw the hospital coroner carrying a body bag to his van, while a police officer handed Sanchez an evidence bag.

Bryan shouted to Ray, "Emma's the mastermind behind the murders. At least in Albuquerque. She's on the run and dangerous!"

Chapter Forty-Five

The Search for Emma

*E*MMA DISAPPEARED. *IT WAS* easy for her with all the chaos and people dealing with another murder at the zoo. Later her car was found abandoned and the home she'd purchased years earlier was emptied of all personal items. She was on the run and had planned for it.

Ray updated Bryan on the murdered volunteer. "We'll have the coroner's report later tomorrow, same with most of the forensics. The zoo will have to remain closed for several days. Perez and other security guards will keep the press off the grounds, and Deidre will give them a brief statement for now. Only the zookeepers and security will be allowed in. And, of course, Miranda... when she's ready."

It had been a hair-raising time between Emma's threats and what looked like a hungry lion roaring at them. "Ray, give me a minute." Bryan went over to Miranda, softly talking to her, his concern apparent. "I'm so sorry. I know you and Emma were friends. But to be honest with you, I was tempted to grab her and toss her into the lions' cage."

Miranda hugged him, "I love you too."

He just held her tight, it said it all.

Emma had to be found, no telling what she was going to do.

In the meantime, Jacob called to tell him, "Fish and I are going to follow up with some people back east who might be able to help find her. Extra police here would be a good idea."

Bryan and Ray didn't comment... or object.

But Emma had no intention of making it easy. She had the same connection as the Powells and had a passport and driver's license with a different name. She changed the color of her hair, wore big reading glasses, and drove to the Denver airport in an old car she had purchased months earlier. She felt as if she was living her life full circle. She knew it would only be a matter of time before someone figured out who she really was.

On a burner cell phone, she called her mother early in the morning before boarding a plane east. Emma knew her father never got up before noon. "I want to see you. Decide when and where we can meet. I'll call you this time tomorrow." She could feel her mother's sadness and broken heart every time she spoke to her.

Emma usually called her mother a couple times a year, always from a phone or place no one could trace. It was a horrible situation, but they had to be very careful in order to protect themselves. It was the only way they would survive. Her father was a monster.

The next morning, her mother told her where they could meet. She would say she was going grocery shopping. It was a gloomy, humid, overcast east coast day— weather Emma had not experienced since she was a teenager. Her heart was pounding. It had been so many years since she had seen her mother. They had been too afraid to chance it. They knew how vicious her father would be if he found out. He would hurt both of them.

Now it didn't matter. She was over it. Everything he was and everything he demanded of Emma was over.

When she saw her mother, their hugs and tears couldn't wipe away the pain she felt when she saw how emaciated her mother was.

Most women abused by men for some absurd reason believe it's their fault when they get angry and violent. Far too many are afraid to leave. Years earlier, Emma had taken the step with her mother's help. Many times, she tried to get her mother to leave, but the abuse and fear had left her emotionally incapable of taking that huge step.

They spoke inside a small neighborhood food shop for over an hour. "Emma, can I see you again tomorrow? Please?" Emma couldn't refuse her, even though she knew time was running out for her being safe. People were looking for her.

"I'll call you early again." Emma held her tight.

On the fourth day since she disappeared from the zoo, they planned to meet again.

This time it was different.

Her father figured something was going on and followed her mother. Smacking her, almost knocking the elderly woman to the ground, he laughed, "What makes you two think you can outsmart me? Stupid women!"

"What about me? Do you want to smack me too? After all these years, you still hit a helpless woman." The old man froze. He would recognize the voice anywhere. Now *he* was experiencing fear.

Jacob quietly walked over and firmly grabbed the old, ugly, miserable man by the arm and steered him toward his car. "Let's take a ride. Some people want to see you."

Emma's mother stood there paralyzed. She'd had too many years of abuse to care. But if anyone had really noticed, they would have seen a slight smile on her face.

Emma still had enough survival instincts to run away through streets still somewhat familiar to her. She ran before Jacob or Fish, who was with him, could grab her. Truth be told, it was her father they wanted the most.

Jacob and Fish had made calls to some people back east after Emma disappeared, people they had known since they were all much younger. Arriving back east the day after Emma did, they were told, "Follow Emma's mother." Their contact didn't say how they knew... but they were right.

"When you find him, bring him to us. We didn't realize he was having people murdered and threatening to get money from you and Leonard. We've let him alone. He never seemed to be doing much harm back here. His family was grateful he had a mistress, so he was rarely home. Sure sorry for his daughter. Jacob, leave him with us."

"Let me know if you find Emma," Jacob told his old friend. "We're going home tomorrow."

Chapter Forty-Six

Four Days and A Lifetime

*F*OR MIRANDA, THE SEARCH for Emma seemed like a lifetime. Extra police were guarding her home day and night. Bryan kept checking in, while still working with Ray to search for her.

Leonard had also called Miranda to be sure she was safe, promising he would see her soon.

One evening when Bryan stopped over, Miranda told him and Isabella about her meeting with Emma before they went to the lions' habitat. "It was so bizarre. Emma kept checking her phone every few minutes, then getting up and walking way. When she came back, her face was flushed, and she seemed anxious. When I asked her if she was feeling okay, she said she had a headache, no big deal. But it was. She had just murdered the volunteer. Which, of course, I didn't know at that time."

"We were in the café for a short time, discussing the expansion plans when Emma literally jumped up and said, 'Let's check on the lions.' Well, you know the rest. You found me and she's disappeared." Miranda let out a big sigh.

"I hope to hell you never scare me like that again." As Bryan reached over to hug her, his phone rang.

"Emma's dead."

The search for Emma was over when Jacob called Anderson with the news.

"Really? How did it happen? And where the hell are you?" Bryan had a pretty good idea.

"What does it matter, Detective? I didn't kill her. She killed herself."

"Who found her body?" Bryan knew there was a lot more to this story.

Ignoring the question Jacob said, "She left a letter. It said, 'forgive me.'"

"And when will I see the letter?" Bryan was sure Jacob was back east.

"Soon," said Jacob and then hung up.

Chapter Forty-Seven

The Sadness in the Letter

*H*ER SUICIDE NOTE WAS a letter of sadness and regret.

He threatened to kill my mother and sisters if I didn't do what he told me to. I hadn't seen or spoken to him in years. I had changed my name to Parker, my mother's maiden name. No one ever questioned me because her last name was on my birth certificate.

They hadn't been married yet when I was born. My mother and two sisters remained in his abusive and destructive world. They were too frightened by his threats to leave. I ran away when he was on a business trip. I was eighteen, and my mother gave me five hundred dollars, which had taken her years to save from grocery money.

She paid dearly for it with two broken ribs and more. His cruelty had no bounds. I knew from what I had experienced. Those kinds of horrible memories and experiences live with you your entire life. My hatred for him and fear of him never left me.

Moving west I felt was far enough away to be safe. I worked all kinds of jobs while I got a degree in communication at the University of Denver. A friend and I drove to Albuquerque one weekend. I loved it and looked for a job. I saw the ad for assistant curator at the zoo. I was confident I could do the job. I had always loved animals. Eventually I became curator and Miranda, who was one of the veterinarians, became the senior vet. We became good friends. In so many ways, it was a wonderful time for me. Then he found me.

I'm not sure how. It doesn't really matter. I think maybe it had something to do with the people in Madrid who were trying to start their new gambling business. Almost a year ago, he called. When I heard his voice, I was so panicked I could hardly breathe. He screamed telling me what he wanted me to do and, if I didn't, he again promised he would kill my mother and sisters. I knew he meant it.

He said he was sending some people to help me do what he asked, and you pretty much know the rest. Two murders at the zoo, fake pieces of paper stuffed in their mouths. The idiot Powell brothers who killed them also killed Karla and attempted to kidnap Miranda. I murdered the volunteer found in the zoo surgery room. She was one of the people he sent to help me. I'd had enough.

For months, I was making my plans to run away. When my father heard the Powell brothers were arrested, he went crazy making all kinds of threats. I said yes to whatever he wanted, even though I believed it was all over. I decided to go back east to see my mother at least one more time. I also planned to kill my father.

Tell my mother I love her, and I've left a will. My money and home go to her and my sisters.

Miranda, I'm so sorry. You deserved a better friend. Forgive me.

Emma

Jacob handed Miranda a copy of the suicide letter he had given Detective Anderson at the police station.

"Who found her body?" The detective was skeptical. He didn't know if he believed it was true.

But it was.

"The police found her and the note in her hotel room. She's dead, Bryan. You can check with them. She called the police to tell them where to find her, then shot herself."

"What about her father, who started this whole mess?"

"How should I know?" Jacob raised his eyebrows, turned, and left the station. Fish and Leonard were waiting in the car for him.

They all knew.

So what!

***

The next day, the news in New Mexico reported a story about the sordid behavior of State Senator Matthew Graham. "Graham has been accused of arranging the murder of his longtime associate Carl Reed. Police say they have proof of his involvement, and he will be arraigned in court later in the week. He has resigned without comment."

Chapter Forty-Eight

The Zoo

"*KAMALI AND HER CUBS,* Imani (meaning faith) and Sabrina, are with their proud father Kasi. Visit the zoo. Bring your camera. They are adorable and not the least bit camera shy. Several more babies are expected. Stay tuned!"

The zoo's re-opening announcement was intended to turn the media focus away from the murders and to the lion cubs and baby zebra. Miranda, Deidre, and George, along with the animal keepers and many volunteers had kept the zoo running. They managed to oversee the daily operation of the zoo and medical care of the animals, as well as the search for a new curator.

George had expressed some concern. "Are you sure someone Emma knew might not show up here?"

"Tell George adding a few more security guards is probably not a bad idea if it would help him feel better but there is nothing to worry about," Bryan had gone to the zoo to reassure them.

"Should we be worried?"

Bryan put his arm around her. "No, just cautious."

"*You know you really like each other—a lot!*" said Agatha, always pushing for romance.

Bryan had reached out to Jacob asking him what he

215

thought about any possible revenge from recent events. "None!"

"You're sure? Those kinds of people have long, mean memories."

"Bryan, I'm very sure. During the last conversation with them they told me there's nothing to worry about anymore. We made sure it's over! Mostly, it's a bunch of old men now who have a hard time getting out of bed in the morning, let alone anything more strenuous."

Isabella and Miranda talked about what a tragedy it was for Emma. The Powell brothers and their cousin would spend years in jail for the murders at the zoo and of Karla. All because of one old man's pathological behavior. And the man being Emma's father was almost too horrible to comprehend.

***

"I have to make a decision about the zoo."

"It may be time to move on," commented Raymond.

"Absolutely," added Sherlock.

"Isabella take a ride with me, I want to show you something," said Miranda.

It was a vacant building located near both the Albuquerque Sawmill Market and Rail Yards Market. They were less than ten minutes from each other near Old Town and Rio Grande Boulevard.

"What do you think?" Miranda asked.

"What do I think about what?" Isabella was smiling. She already had a pretty good idea.

"I want to open my own animal care center. After all that's happened at the zoo, I need to move on... a new beginning of sorts."

"Do you have the money to get started?" Isabella knew she would say yes even if she didn't.

"Mostly. What I don't have, I'll borrow from the bank. Plus, the consulting fee from the Bishop's project at the Rescue Center will help. I'm pretty excited about it!"

"Forget the bank. I'll make a great silent partner."

The women hugged knowing it would work.

The sense of hopefulness and possibilities it gave them was exactly what they needed to move beyond the ugliness of murders and murderers, of the sadness from loss.

Chapter Forty-Nine

Love Is a Puppy and a Kiss

MONTHS LATER, THE CLINIC was lit up in celebration of the opening of Dr. Miranda Scott's Veterinarian Animal Care Services. The empty building had been renovated and the doctor and her staff ready to see patients.

There was much to be thankful for this night.

Ray Sanchez brought his pregnant wife. He would be taking the detective test soon. He laughingly handed Miranda their good luck gift. So appropriate, the popular Raymond Chandler black and white films, *The Big Sleep* and *Farewell My Lovely*.

"We heard you love these types of films."

"I certainly do," thinking how grateful she was the voices in her head were being quiet this night!

The dear, sweet Bishop's showed up with two large, framed photos of beautiful horses.

Isabella announced her children's books writing programs at Albuquerque libraries, and they had put a shelf with her books on it in a corner of the waiting room.

Her father and Jacob purchased the building for them as a gift. It wasn't so bad having retired gangsters for relatives... as long as they stayed retired!

Leonard Scott also came and, after giving his daughter a big hug. introduced her to an attractive Native American woman. "Miranda, this is my wife, Sakari."

"Why did you have to go into hiding? I've been so worried about you. And where did you meet this lovely woman?"

"Another time sweetheart, I promise. What about you and Bryan?"

Miranda just kissed her father on the check, "I love you."

Bryan whispered to Isabella, walked out, and came back in with the most special gift of all. Handing Miranda the leash to an Australian Shepherd puppy he said, "Your new watch dog." And giving her a big kiss, he whispered, "You know, I love you."

The detective and the veterinarian were too busy to deal with the "I love you" issue for now but… eventually they would.

Of course, the voices had to have their say.

"*Yes, you can trust him.*" Agatha was such a romantic.

"*Well, we agree!*" chimed in Sherlock and Raymond.

"What are you going to name her?" asked Bryan.

With a mischievous grin Miranda said, "Agatha."

Epilogue

Time to Carry a Gun?

*A**S THE SUN ROSE* over the southwest, Dr. Miranda Scott was on her way to an emergency at the clinic. The early morning sky was colored with wide shades of purple and pink blending together once full daylight appeared.

Hot air balloons often took flight at dawn on cool mornings like this. She saw nearly a dozen of them as she went to meet an anxious client bringing in a four-year-old white lab stuck in labor.

Miranda had texted one of her technicians to meet her. Everyone on staff took turns being on call for emergencies. They happened often. An animal hit by a car, a dog losing a fight with another dog, or porcupine quills stuck in its furry body. Pneumonia was common, as were young animals brought to them filled with parasites, having been mistreated in a puppy mill. Feral kittens saved from all sorts of places needed care. And there were pets, mostly older ones, suffering from arthritis or cancer.

"The saddest and hardest part of my job is having to put down an animal who has been a beloved pet and seeing the owners say goodbye to them, their hearts broken by the loss," Dr. Scott told a reporter who interviewed her when she first opened the clinic.

Within an hour, the doctor and technician helped deliver five healthy pups. Two others unfortunately did not survive. It was a little after 7:00 a.m. The clinic usually opened at 8:30.

The waiting area and treatment rooms had large photos of animals covering the walls, including the ones of horses from Ruthie and Garrett Bishop, now major patrons of the Southwest Rescue and Retirement Center.

The clinic's large front windows, which had been tinted to block the hot sun during the day, did not block people from staring inside. Usually, it was not a problem. Today was different.

Agatha, the Australian Shepard puppy Bryan gave Miranda as a gift when she opened her practice, had grown to twice its size already and, although still a bouncing baby, her growl could easily scare unwanted visitors. Once the lab, the puppies, and their owner left, Agatha was barking and pawing at one of the large front windows.

His face pressed again the window startled Miranda. He ran away. She knew it was him.

She was sure it was him. Miranda called her father.

"I'm pretty sure I saw Uncle Douglas minutes ago. His face was staring in the window of my clinic. Isn't he in jail for murder?"

"He didn't escape. He was released. Call your boyfriend. I'm on my way." Leonard hung up.

"Yes, of course, call Bryan. Now!" Agatha sounded worried.

Sherlock and Raymond were once again in agreement and together shouted, *"Hurry!"*

Miranda called Bryan and waited for him and her father, remembering the stories she had been told about her uncle. Four years younger than his brother Leonard, Douglas was not the baby of the family, although he acted it. They had a younger sister who had been living in Paris all her adult life. But that was another story!

In and out of trouble and jail for years, Douglas was often more trouble than he was worth according to his wife. Even with all his con games and scams, they never had much money. Their marriage was a disaster from the start. Six weeks after they were married, he was arrested for pawning stolen jewelry. Still, she stayed in the loveless and childless marriage. She was a sad and defeated woman. We've all met men and women like that, unable to move beyond their past.

Seriously abused as a young girl, its devastating effects lingered her whole life. When she had been told to leave him, she would reply, "Where do I have to go?" When she was told he had another wife, her comment was, "Let her have the bastard." She died alone while he was in prison this last time. It was a sad end to a truly sad life.

Leonard Scott knew anything to do with his brother could only mean trouble, although he had never really been dangerous. He also never believed Douglas committed the murder he was accused of.

Bryan arrived five minutes before Leonard. Of course, he does have a police car with a siren!

"He was released from prison two weeks ago. Apparently, his lawyers were able to prove he wasn't guilty for some reason or other and couldn't possibly have committed the murder."

Leonard walked in and heard Bryan and asked, "Well, what's he done now?"

"Unfortunately, we have reason to believe he's involved in some trouble here."

"Meaning?"

"Leonard, he's a person of interest. I can't tell you why."

"Is there a warrant out for his arrest?"

"Yes!"

But what Bryan wanted to know was, "Do you think he would hurt Miranda?"

"I doubt it. He was always very fond of her. Still, I don't know what he's liable to do or what he wants. You need to find him and ask him!" Leonard was clearly frustrated and concerned for his daughter.

"Did he try to get into the clinic? Was he banging on the window?" Bryan asked.

"No. He was just staring in and ran away when he realized I saw him."

"Leonard, do you have any idea where he might go?"

"It's been a long time since I've heard from him. He knew after years of helping and supporting him, I refused to do it anymore."

Bryan texted Ray to meet him at the station and pull up any files he could find on Douglas Scott.

Several people were waiting outside the clinic with their pets along with the rest of the staff. There were now two vet technicians, an office manager, and scheduler to coordinate the flow of patients and surgery appointments.

"We'll be fine. Go, both of you. See, lots of people will be around me all day." Miranda hugged each of the men in her life and unlocked the clinic's door.

"Let me know when you're done for the day. I'll bring dinner." Bryan walked out and held the door open for a very large woman with a very large dog who was limping. As Miranda turned to walk into a treatment room with the woman and her dog, she saw Bryan talking to her father who was shaking his head yes.

At the station, Sanchez handed Anderson the information he wanted. It included a couple photos of Douglas Scott, along with his record as a con man, jewel thief, and bigamist.

"Bigamist? I can't figure out how to get married once!" Anderson burst out laughing.

Sanchez couldn't resist. "Maybe he can share his secret to marital bliss with you?"

"Cute! Advice from you or the Scott family of gangsters and criminals is just what I need. I couldn't fall in love with someone from a Mormon family!"

"Hey, I want to be invited to your wedding... if it ever happens. Should I bring handcuffs? Sanchez was laughing and truly enjoying himself.

At the clinic Miranda was not enjoying herself, wondering if she should be scared of this man she hadn't seen in over a dozen years. What did he want peering in her window early this morning?

Leonard Scott and his small group of merry men, Jacob and Fish—well, really retired gangsters—decided on their own actions. They knew a thing or two about bad guys.

Bryan didn't trust Leonard completely and arranged for a police officer to follow him. Like Leonard wouldn't realize it! For now, no one could find Douglas.

Was Douglas Scott dangerous?

The Scott family and close associates seemed to once again be involved in criminal matters. In the meantime, if only they knew.

Miranda saw him in the rearview mirror as she drove home. Douglas was hiding in the back seat of Miranda's car. Another skill of his... breaking into cars!

All three of her famous voices were in agreement.

"Sweetheart, you could be in for trouble, again. Maybe it's time you carry a gun!"

AUTHOR'S NOTE

There are some 350 zoos in the United States, and it's estimated that well over 600 million people visit them each year.

The first public zoo in the United States opened in 1874 in New York City and was called the Central Park Zoo. Many of the first animals donated to the zoo came from famous Americans, including President Abraham Lincoln, Samuel Morse, August Belmont, General William Sherman, and General George Custer.

The oldest running zoo in the world is the Vienna Zoo in Schonbrunn which dates from 1752.

The first modern zoo was built in 1793, in Paris, France and located in the Ménagerie du Jardin des Plantes. The zoo is a part of Paris's Jardin des Plantes (botanical garden) that opened way back in 1635.

There are a number of organizations and foundations worldwide dedicated to the proper care and treatment of animals in zoos. Most offer programs to provide understanding and education about the animals, as well as the importance of breeding programs designed to prevent the extinctions of any species. Visit and support your local zoo!

"The Incredible Dr. Pol" is a delightful program on *National Geographic Wild*. They show great care and kindness to animals large and small as do several other similar programs.

Located next to the Rio Grande in Albuquerque, New Mexico, the 64-acre zoo opened in 1927. There are more than 1,000 animals and 270 species. For a full day of fun, visit the zoo, aquarium, and botanic gardens, located at the Albuquerque Biological Park. There is a gift shop and food vendors are located throughout the park.

I hope I will be forgiven for making this wonderful zoo (of which I am a member) the site of my recent murder mystery.